SPITESTAMENT

a blaxploitation manifesto

by

DuVay Knox

SPIT (verb): Utter in a Hostile or Aggressive
way.

TESTAMENT (noun): an expression of
conviction or creed.

----

i wood be remiss if i did not say this is mah truth that eye speek to u as proof in da nigga figga vernaculistick language n tongue for those old & young for wich i have aimed n framed these valiant n salient werds to be heard or read instead since im nyet yet dead and that bee this: mah choices in life have been mah own & da consequences of mah actions have been borne by mee wit da expressed/unnerstanding/innerstanding & overstanding that everythang that has happened to mee was of mah own free will. I Am A Free Agent. Yet-though life has bestowed such agency upon mee it has not prevented mee from making gross errors of judgement that resulted in unwanted attention from the natural forces of the universe. For bee it known that nature abhors a vacuum & so seeks to fill any unbalance created by a Mans bad decisions. The tenet of entropy being what it is one can not undo ones mistake n science continues to err in this regard to realize it into concrete. Butt when it is understood that the scientifik seekers can not be awakened to such truths due to the dominance of the Powers That Be upon their minds this makes it clear why the world continues to be under false teachings across the spectrum of knowledge. And it is against this monolith that I suffered at length upon standing up to the tyranny of evil of The Terrorists of Humanity who were never pleased in their tastes with my sound rite reasoning of their politics that tended to unravel in lite of the solidity of my logical compositions that nullified their alleged deep learning. True their objecktions contained a sertain method that appeared to cum korrect butt upon closer inspection and for sho retrospection the seams of their arguments were shown to be mere threads leading no where butt in a circle. And as one hoo was responsible for exposing the futility of their equations and the dubious nature of said phenomena a nigga such as i became persona non grata which is to say my ass wasnt welcum in any hierarchal intellectual environments where a kool head such as mines would prevail over the bullshit passing for brains and the detritus passing for thinking. Of course it doesnt help that in such situations i never deigned to hold those of that ilk in reverence despite the opulence we found ourselves holding court in especially so as i aged finding that respect for the wrongful is just as deleterious to ones psyche as disrespect for the righteous causing genuine havoc to ensue in both instances in a manner similar to karma on steroids or payback as a muthafucka which if u kan help it u never want to bring that level of balancing the scale into your own life at the behest of your own doing butt alas as i have said earlier in this missive i injured mahself with my proclivities yet I hold no ill will for were it not for these nigga lessons I would not be hoo I am at this writing to pass along to you these valuable insites n hindsites of posterior reminisces that I hope serve as fertile fodder for your own moovements and groovements with such antagonists you may also cum up against in your wheelings n dealings especially with those of the church institutions universities medical industrial complex federal governments racist whitey crackers coons samboes negroids and enemies known and unknown that I know not by a particular name at this very moment butt u shall know them when u see them or cum upon them or they enter your life at precisely the moment they wanna start sum shit butt having read these werds u will be able to end that same shit and send it back frum whence it came and kontinue to stand against those hoo would rigorously try to suppress you via spurious means therefore I doo my best to speak a riotous language of the often unheard which tends to be real niggaz such as mahself no matter if they think it absurd and perhaps even u if u are reading this that we may stay fortified in a vanishing world of careless morals where those hoo consider themselves the mighty steady create desolate hoods across amerikkka by way of intrigue and subterfuge then point the finger at niggaz as cause and effect all the while concealing the blood on their hidden hands they use to shuffle paperwork that disappears whole communities of niggaz at the stroke of midnite at the end of a fiscal year in and out without a doubt or hesitation and this is bizness as usual using voodoo economics because niggaz sole reason for existing according to white folks is for us not to multiply butt die and become the statistics that make cities famous for tourism dollars because peeple wanna cum and see where mike brown died for example on the ground frum bullets made in serbia croatia ukraine by ruffians hoo are descendants of an ancient regime used to assisting in the deaths of the unfortunates and so i ask u not to take this as a meager summary or mere lamentation butt more of a jeremiad screed polemic or manifesto of an absolute werk that

refrains not frum direct confrontation nor
any deluge of personal assault it may
engender for i cum not in peace butt wit a
2-edged sword to stop the plot of nobles
against niggaz hoo dont realize how noble
they are so that the manipulative
machinations may not succeed in devouring
our existence nor dehydrating our essence
and to that end I am not meant to be impartial
or even reasonable with my telling the frank
truth the whole nigga truth so help me niggod
for what is a man without truth in his life
butt a liar waiting to be dug up and exposed
as mere shadow rather than actual factual
flesh of man deserving to be validated with
authenticity of the enemy and the enemy of
our enemy and within those werds a
revelatory strategy for intuiting the nature
of ones foes that be those hoo pose often as
friends yet butt are really howling wolves
imitating lambs while leading sheeple to
slaughter this being how they accelerate the
demise wit no chance of renewal only removal
of those they dont want to be round just to
pound in the ground where the bodies will be
found to abound this is Y my constant vigil is
for u to gird your loins and protect ya neck
that your intelligence be illuminated by the
torch of these werds that your soul be guided
by my inflammatory assessments of these
realizations even as we strive to exist in
occupied territory. For we know there is no
such thang as justice wit these kind that rule
because in their purview and under their
review justice is actually revenge since they
see themselves as the lords of the manor
meting out manners to make the knaves behave
n measure up thus these discourses in lieu of

4

the society in wich we live in today will be
likely accused by lame amateurs of being
alien rhetorick of a lunatick mind whose
speech should not be trusted rather than
being understood for the times we are living
in for wich they are written yet the fack
remains truly that these thoughts are not
mere emotional unstable drivel but
retaliatory justifications in line with the
declaration of war on mah person and mah
peeple whose physikal value has been
appointed for destruction and i therefore
knowing this within my being knew that the
day had arrived when self had to tell the
truth on self in order that the treasures of
righteousness be unlocked that hold the key
to saving ones self and loved ones hoo
wannabe saved for we know that sum kan be
saved while others dont wannabe saved frum
even themselves let alone the enemy of man.
Meanwhile the many of the rest of the best of
the niggaz i know are by n by on standby and
have been for a long time waiting for this
stone cold knowledge you caint git in college
to drop frum mah humble blunt darkened lips
which are dedicated to parting to spit fire
that becums a conflagration that endures in
your heart as an enthusiasm for secrets that
exist between n around the werds as they lay
on the page frum a sage such as mahself and
what must be gleaned frum them will only be
seen by those of you hoo are the true natural
heirs of this salvo of kabalistical doctrinal
intellectual info that be a testament to all
that has been shewn a nigga in his
industrious time upon earth dealing wit
racist white folks also known as crackers hoo
knowing of me will always wish to condemn me

and mah rap as mere pap or want mee limping
to stop mah pimping which tho it aint easy
must go on until the break of dawn cuz real
pimping never stops or sleeps no matter hoo
has a mind to cum up against it because im
rubber you are glue & whatever u say bounces
off of me n sticks to you is one of the
foundational laws of self preservation frum
the time we were shawties and caint be broken
wit weak playa platitudes nor attitudes on
the level therefore nuthing you do shall
prosper when u try to cum up against me and
mines whether it be indiscreetly or
discriminately. Furthermore built into this
lingua franca is a self protective mechanism
geared to be self destructive in the hands of
the unworthy because they will be seen as
undeclared to such and will not account for
much accordingly to the evil ambitious
immoral man hoo will not find solace in this
occult mystery scripture imparted in the form
as it is written for the proper absorption by
the chosen ones of real niggaz bloodstream
outside of this it will remain an esoteric
impenetrable treatise as it must til i rust
reincarnate or return frum my ferry across
that great river rowing wit stix spoken about
by a legion of big mama nem upon their death
at the hands usually of a cystem that uses em
for experimentation without pity concern or
consternation in the unruly universe they
populate as heads of state pretending loyalty
to the hoi polloi butt its only to royalty on
high hoo allow them to distribute punishment
to those they select to die for no other reason
than they can git away with it and so this
constantly takes place as bizness as usual tho
its unusual wit the perusal ending in

violence both expressed and implied frum those hoo have lied to divide and conquer and kill at will. Altho u may not take me at my werd since i am the one writing this i still advise u not to miss the value n fidelity of my forthrite fervid faithful testimony conveyed here which may even be mah memoirs of the wars of life for these are mah views on white supremacist-thinking men and traitorous inferior-thinking negroids hoo assisted them in the downfall of niggaz that should be considered a glaring warning record of charlatans described here and how they operate in their hallowed halls in profligacy and crime wit caucasity audacity not sagacity and without regard to retribution or hueman life since they kontrol the beast that is babylon bent forever on a mission to stifle spiritual evolution of niggaz in a lewd illusion of inclusion grafted into the thawt process that blots n rots the thinking frum the inside out as it acts as an unstable electron which causes deprivation thru oxidation and suffering in a body that is still alive yet rendering it non existent in a fate worse than death for such a man or woman or child hoo often bears the brunt of the parents fuck ups thus becumming a slave the moment it is born to be ruled by subversion n perversion in this thang called life rife with dark days teetering on the abyss of annihilation for which this country loves to ready unmarked graves for niggaz such as we and thereby remoove us as head of households in hoods across amerikkka. Nevertheless this old body im in has and will remain steadfast in the fight for the upliftment of niggaz so that my purpose will be fulfilled as it was written long ago before i was born so that it may be so and i will have earned my right to retire to the eden of mah eternal rest but while alive i am built to run and never git tired and mount a campaign that will never git tedious even when entertaining these devils directly hoo have stayed vigilant in desiring to bring about my complete ruin that while it has not yet happened therein did manage indeed to cause me a number of misfortunes as i have mentioned in the foregoing wit my eviction frum the good times being the consequence of those actions yet overall their attempt at vicious victory has been impotent. Butt such is the nature of the devil in the flesh that is Ethnick Enemies of all stripes whose stripes nor spots will never change nor behavior which is embedded deep within their psyches and shall not be removed under any circumstances for it was forged by environmental pressures unlike any for the niggaz hoo were indigenous aborigines to the topsoil of earth first and foremost as the first hueman life to be on the land periodt walking uprite having erections to produce more beings long before the superior-minded crackkka showed up and showed his ass to brang calamity n destroy peace that had been upon alla niggaz for centuries prior to his alabaster arrival. And having found those such as i hoo refuse to accept his compensations or lock step with his shenanigans the enemy wich is now the poisoned of all races has consistently been prompted to prosecute many of our nigga race as a matter of abysmal principle as is his stile simply on the strength of spreading pain and committing heinousness without

8

consolation is how he moves and has being never even once contemplating sound morals as a characteristic of a civilized nature which understandably the mouf of the villainous housing a forked tongue disgusts me to the point of spittin in the face of his wayward yet time honored philosophies cuz I dare be that muthafucka hoo knows i done earned the rite to speek about this fite against the mite of evil and these scars on my ass serve as proof that i have been more than willing to go toe to toe n blow for blow and give an eye for an eye toof for toof for troof so that even tho parts of my soul are missing and my physikal aint what it useta be thanks to my mental im still unbowed n unmooved mah niggaz much to do with the niggods sustaining my hands upon the keys of this machine as i write this in rage i still rise each and every day to face the sway of the prevailing winds sweeping molehills and mountain tops with influential programming doing a great damage to most of our peeples. Yet i for one have restrained mahself from being reduced to tears of sadness or groveling n wallowing in my own shit in a woe is me pose cuz i knows not suppose that its not mah way to be weak or meek to gain sympathy frum the massa for sum perceived benefit of the establishment knowing damn well that a Nigga of mah ilk wont wilt n would rather hang by the neck until dead than profane the secrets of the real niggahood that bonds me with the few of u hoo are left hoo are of a fearless disposition and now peep this joint i write in exile frum a hood sumwhere in amerikkka. Sum among u may want to follow in mah footsteps thus much of what i have to say

here in these pages is about this journeys
lonely trek a reminder that broad is the way
of lames simps n suckaz butt narrow is the
road on which real authentic muthafuckaz
hussle n bussle because not many want or kan
handle the sorrows of morrows that often cum
to visit n sit on a nigga shoulder as a
limitation and sprinkle grief on ones plans
in a constant attempt of deterrence to keep u
wretched and your eyes off the prize so be
mindful as u read that only the strong
survive the falsehoods and no goods n manage
to stay at a high estate in any state because
we know how to be firmly grounded on the
correct principles of Game. This be krucial to
the conflicks u will have to endure frum
those tossing much manure your way to stick
to u as paste to shut your stinking mouf so u
are marked by the stench as a pariah rendered
mute by hue and outcry so u will be incapable
of speech and seen as a deluded kind of
something wit hatred on your name so be
brought to an end and it does not matter how
it is done as long as its done and you or i fall
to an aggressive campaign of contemptible
wickedness because men hoo rule are always
ecstatic when those hoo dare stand up to them
are fell as trees in the forest and no one
hears them fall so they hoo be as barbarous as
they wannabe kan sit around chopping it up
about   your   destruction   without
konsternation. They love the feel it gives
them to rid the world of peeple like u or i hoo
have been stamped as Real Niggaz so its a
joyous occasion for them to kill our Figgaz
thus this way they kan be sure others will not
be enriched by posterity wit what we have
done nor will generations forever afterwards

10

hear about how we putt in that werk so i urge
u not to be the type of muthafucka hoo buries
his or her talent or squander your werds on
pigs hoo cant hear shit nor do they wanna
hear the werds that are cumming forth frum
your mouf that have never been spit in such a
fashion because since u prolly like me have
been entreated with a gift of the gab u are
ruining the stile and image most are used to
and your very presence is meant to brang shit
out frum its hiding place due to the fack that
whats long been hidden must be brought to the
lite of reasoning even as the enemies attempt
to throw shade to try and stop a type of truth
heretofore never heard before by others.
Remember it must never be forgotten that we
are at war behind enemy lines because an
undeclared war has been declared on niggaz
in attitude of quietude using an abundance of
caution via a racist anarchist algoriddim
made for a database of ruin which takes note
of our customs habits n voices for a program
of ready violence to make us afraid and to
embed fear thru their veritable institutions
n religions so we will conform out of
perceived necessity or tremble out of respect
for divinity thereby genuflecting to ghosts
or personages characteristic of all military
outfits since we are butt in a military
society quiet as its kept butt jesus wept as
many dont seem to notice that we are rank and
file citizens for godamn sho thus they are
looking for the peeple hoo r sheeple willing
to think they are diligently dying for god
and country when its really just government
and corporation under a military banner aka
flag. So let these clues occupy a position in
your mind as salient sagacious sentences and

if there be errors in mah writing they are
surrounded by such righteous pertinency as
to insure no body gits hurt because they are
of a non injurious nature yet they are bombs
to those they are meant to convict as my
gumption intuits this presumption of their
meritorious content finding honor among the
rite niggaz hoo will be properly triggered
and know how to massage them for ingenuity
purposes in this korrupted corona covid age
we are now in. For bear in mind that the
contempt for poverty that the heralded of
babylon have for it is one which makes them
hypocrites because they arranged the socio
economic conditions for it to thrive n
survive as an animal to devour the poor and
then question the victims of the outcum as the
culprits in order to give them a trial by fire
to find them guilty of being hungry which is
a sin in a starving society punishable by
death or misunderstanding because it needs
to be made clear that a starving man has no
independent conscience when his stomack is
touching his back frum lack of food which
inevitably leads to bitter irreconcilable
feuds with the weaker of those he must prey
upon in a dog eat dog world that has been
transformed frum a god feed god world. So
knowing this i have no problem or
compunction regards giving offence to the
oppressive powerful that be wit what is being
said here for your eyes n ears sumtimes thru
mah tears butt not because im sad butt because
im glad i know nuthing kan stop a real nigga
whose time has cum and this is that hour for
the cause of payback/slayback and i kare not
so much for my own being to wit i embrace mah
exposure   to   the   nonsense   immense

12

immeasurable hatred of the haters prevaricators n manipulators. So as well let there be no doubt about those i discuss herewith since the opportunity has now presented itself whereby our ill intentions kan be used as ancient alchemical beneficial magick to condemn the actions of the allied alined haters inside erry race hoo 2getha are the incorrigible enemy led by Crackkaz and those among our own hoo have cold blooded sided with them and mind u i dont say what i have said here out of pure mirth or humor altho that u will find within this literary delivery butt i kno what so ever i speak of frum a long constant study and observation of Crackkkaz human affairs and of those hoo do their bidding as snitches n traitors frum among our own peeple yet again i say those real niggaz among u will know how to receive n perceive this missive and be not dismissive which i pity would be a massive mistake to konsider mah screed an unworthy friend of yo ears thereby failing to make the most of these golden insites into the tripe nature of crackkkaz n samboes whose stank ways were implanted in me to peep n understand frum mah birth frum the niggar constellation of stars that came to earth to rest in the soil that then automated to create all of us and after a time sum among us mahself included evolved a certain kind of chromosomic consciousness that refused tyranny oppression enslavement obedience poverty and of course this is a thankless route to undertake in the wake of others who evolved to be diabolikal in dispensing trubble n tribulation to hem mah mouf so i would never say anything again against their slickery and trickery. Butt

13

since being defective is not an option in mah
book of life there be those hoo count it
against me and oppose me at every turn to
burn my werds where ever they appear on paper
or elicit frum mah mouf found as notes in the
files of those hoo dared listening to me at
great personal risk for which im thankful for
they have been mah only allies and of sincere
utility in this war of the soul and mama
nature being what she is have blessed n
blissed them as a result so that the message of
the messenger has still been able to permeate
the mental acuities of those hoo had ears to
hear even as fear stalked their spirits with
credible   threats   yet   they   remained
determined not to omit mah thought forms so
to those i say here now that i will never
forgit the noble labors of such real niggaz
brought on mah behalf to renounce the ways of
amerikkka the bruteful while taking heed to
the ancient of days ways of knowledge that i
be dropping that cums frum the bowels of the
ancients hoo reside inside my thinking for
remedy is always to be found and had in the
past decisions of our niggacestor ancestors
that   have   recorded   their   divine   nigga
attributes that is to say DNA within our
melanic bloodstreams as light fight codes so
that if we pay attention especially during
perilous times we kan tap into n tweek our
systems and find opinion for dominion of any
situation or shituation that werries or seeks
to bury obliterate or make us victims of
genocidal   behavior   frum   the   enemy   or
friendnemy with his perpetual uses of
education and religion and media to injure
and   pervade   n   invade   our   bodies   with
psychiatric enneagrams n programs so that we

fall by the wayside and over time there be
nary a good intelligence among our peeple to
extract true meaning frum the bullshit
passing for liberation information due to
incapacitation of the fundamentals that are
now solely detrimental even just a vestige of
what once was great minds belonging to viable
niggaz hoo done been rendered useless now.
Thus i make it known that this is the type of
new world order potent shit i wanna save mah
niggaz frum if they butt wannabe saved
because i understand that the malignant
behavior of many of mah very own peeple has
made it too late for them to ever cum or
return unto the fold again altho they may be
reading mah remarks for themselves they will
be taken by such negroids as shit for flies
and they will thereby not reap the prophetik
profit of mah werds meant to disturb and
thereby discount the distance of the long
road to salvaging freedom and victory over
caucosoid devils and alla ethnoid devils
helpers. Therefore u must keep game innermost
in your thoughts that a new strategy must
ensue that we have to pursue because the
enemy has known well to keep niggaz spread
apart like the opposites leggs of a bitch in
heat or the beasts in the concrete jungles of
various hoods of the united states and being
dispersed in this way security frum this
situation is hazardous to our health n wealth
due to our small numbers at any one location
where we will not be able to withstand any
attacks so we see the cunning genius of
crackkkaz in setting us apart frum each other
while we on the other hand by the many have
been programmed to think progress has been
made due to sumthing called integration

which was just even more separation to make us vulnerable and even werse strangers one brotha to the otha one sista to the otha sowing the distrust among us ever deep thus we stay sleep like a giant gulliver held down by mere midgets hoo if we were to awaken and arise would scatter like roaches when the lite cums on in that white house built by niggaz which is now a trap house of prostitution n so korrupt its hurtful and i guarantee you not promise you that nothing will change going forward therefore we must brang the change and the pain with it where necessary. Because know that we are seen as a transgressive trespassing peeple despite being indigenous aboriginal originals and first peeples of the hereditary land on which we stand now as strangers tho that has been taken over by lustful wanton degenerates across all racial types hoo bee steeped in avarice graft shaft and disrespect hoo loathe u me and we wit a vengeance no matter how rong or unfounded it is their adrenal nature knows only how to be that which always sees life as a struggle of the survival of the fittest even when there is no evidence that a struggle or strife must be engaged in nor when there be no need for war their aggressive regressive r-complex nature still sees war violence brutality n perversity as necessary goodness instead of the evil it is. However balance being the norm of a society is naturally sought out by beneficient forces giving rise to such real niggaz as i hoo came to putt mah foot so far up the ass of the government monarchy which is only anarchy til it cums out the other side and thereby chill them in the license to kill they have

taken out on the peeple holding meetings
using impudent counsel to make pernicious
decisions to exterminate those hoo they see
fit or they determine aint shit so their
choice to form standing armies known
erroneously as police when the truth is cops
are jes boots on the ground to surround
niggaz under the guise of justified
legislation they say is a tolerant
constitution yet we know that when a long
train of abuses and usurpations evinces a
design to reduce Niggaz under absolute
despotism it is Niggaz right it is Niggaz duty
to throw off such government and to provide
new guards for their future security for new
Niggaz cumming after because we no longer
consent to be governed by those hoo dont have
a decent respect for other huemans therefore
such power has to be resolved to be dissolved
and we be disconnected frum them so we kan be
separate equal n balanced again in our own
skins we in and were it not expedient to say
so i would not be saying so butt Crackkkaz
have perpetuously been perpetrating insults
injuries and death to an unheard degree to a
nigga simply on the strength that a nigga
skin color is different frum his and thus he
feels sum kinda way and as a result disposes
us to suffer slings and arrows of outrageous
misfortune in order that he can cum up by
eating off the substance of niggaz and using
our blood in his laboratories to ascend to
immortality which is not based on what i
heard butt what i kno fo sho as i been born to
speak out against this shit that will go on
unless we stop giving our consent via silence
that condones their violence in our lives and
those of our loved ones since they see

themselves lying outside the realm of being able to be korrected where the truth dont apply to them thus they have grown insolent as fuck to the point of being incompatible with honor and the truth aint in em n maybe never was cuz it was all just pretense anyway frum day one when we encountered them fools and thought they was kool when it was just the ice in their veins paving the way for their institutionalized savagery reflected in inner cities not only in amerikkka but across the world even into space a place that is full of debris and commercial advertisements for coca cola and aunt jemima syrup unkle ben rice on the satellites that look up niggaz ass when they use the bathroom n fuck in the bedroom so needless to say i would be remiss if didnt use these werds to cast invectives about their lawless transgressive transactions actions against niggaz. This be about the villainies toward the virtues ever present that scoundrels hoo study war day n nite seek to carry out where ever possible in the form of skemes and skullduggery and god be damned hoo doesnt exist anyway for our peeple purposes like we have been taught since we were brought into n bought into his existence as a friend of niggaz in case we ever needed sumbody greater than them except as far as sertain kinda wayward caucasity is concerned aint nobody greater than them on earth thus they have no konsideration of deity unless it be thim and thus suffers no consequences of their treachery since they be their own judge n jury which means they will never diminish or punish Thimselfs in the eyes of the whole world in the interest of something as foreign as justice cuz there be none for Thim butt for others justice is revenge where they take the reins to mete it out at will so that slaughter massacre n extinction be the result of their hidden hand wit no man to judge thim except me since i have nothing to lose butt mah chains. Because the threats of mah participators haters and accusers against mah life vile tho they may be long ago lost their impack on me so i accept the crown i must wear sumtimes upside down along wit misfortunes and all despairs that cum with it cuz i dont seek the approval of the babylonian barbarians hoo i know love to set u up with a reputation that they kan yank away frum u soon as u becum discordant with their wishes n switches or abandon their prime directives after a fashion strip u of all recognitions they funded because as far they are koncerned its facks u committed sacriligious acks that deserve what ever punishment they choose to fasten to you so that now u are stained in the minds and hearts of those hoo trusted you. Yet many are too dumb to know that u have been unscrupously set up with perjurious receipts and false deceits of the hollywood variety and now yo ass caught out without a defense of yo alleged offense to be banished wit damage to your name and those hoo trusted wondering after u in an atlas cloud of confusion unable to discern divinity frum diabolikalness and forgetting that the fervent desire is to brang an end to human society as a whole the better if its done thru such artifices where the peeple kan be misled in the head. Howsumever if we remember to tap into our souls we kan affect a stance that will withstand even the worst our foes kan throw at us butt this is why niggaz are kept off balance so we will stay outta touch with the atman deeper part of our beings which is that noble perfecktion of us that be in deprivation due to various strategies that makes us foreigners to our own bodies so that we are like the deaf n dumbed down kinda negroids with nothing left butt a degraded life since we are so far remooved frum hoo our peeple once were any attempt at communing with the spirits is lost as a ritual in order that we be able to receive the transmission of the inner mysteries to remain high initiates hoo know how to overthrow the elements and command slaveish ghouls as well as repudiate profane konceptions. Butt numerous of us almost too many of us to count have lost the key to our inner nigga figga that be a sign how powful perchance ignorance is and i have no desire to leave behind no man woman or child to be unfortunate and hoo truly have a thirst for revenge as the true lords of this manor called earth. Then i know this what u read will increase in you a passion to show those hoo have lost their way how to git back to that magickal extraordinary stile thats deep down in our instincts that resides there for the purpose of being called up in the rite nigga way to eradicate the soul disintengrate the bonds frum the enslavement of any enemy when one is in willing accord with the divine obediences of nature. This will happen when the mind wakes up and we pass into a level of consciousness reserved for only the ready ones among us hoo attain an access that will automatically renounce the stranglehood of Crackkka Powerhood & Company frum da hood frum time and space because nothing kan stand up to the divine spark that lites up in niggaz bosom into degrees of initiation full consciousness and evolution into the plane of the niggod body leading to the true destiny of the Real Nigga Race. Nowdays however we be those capable of avoiding superficial meditations and i know this better due to my inner nigga figga cumming to me at a time when i was most distraught about yall after i had just hit the blunt after a bout of deep fucking n sucking where i had the dick up in her stomack muskles and lo she enjoyed it to the utmost cuz i was doing the most with what i had so that by the time of my unlaxing as i lay there in the sweaty amore of the after effect and hit the joint one mo time it came to me forthwith about why the relationship between the black man n woman is so fucked up in this twenty first century millieu that is far away frum where it once was when we ruled amerikkka as a coupled peeple the reason being we were together like ace boon kings n queens wit emphasis on the boon hoo were looking like we would rule forever over a land we discovered before crackkka columbus stole the land and the credik til this very day so that we went frum being land lords to tenants under new tenets of eviction per the contractual obligations of the constitution which was a document made out of parched rolling papers frum the marijuana crops we niggaz had grown under peaceful peacepipe paradisiacal conditions. Butt that all changed when the nigga and his niggress succumbed to the fakes/snakes that invaded their garden of eden/eating and instigated a prevaricated argument that split the black man and woman up so bad that we are still

fighting to the death over it in this exact
moment rather than how we were when neither
one of us was touched by hate n disdain for
the other with endless gazing into each
others eyes cuz the attraction was so strong
we were lovesick in the heart of hearts
without an ounce of hostility that couldnt
even git thru to us to cause calamity seeing
as how there was no effort to our love butt the
trickeries of sertain whiteys n their
multiracial criminal comraderies sumhow
became greater than the black man and womans
loyalty to each other. Thus our hearts got
opened dulled infected n rearranged by
change and before we knew what done happened
boff of us had lost our shit to the point we
forgot the well known paths we had traveled
to arrive at the place in each others whole
soul that was keeping us as one therefore we
currently sit in error in this era searching
for a cure for a disease that will remain
incurable if we dont pay heed to how the game
is played with charms that are used to harm n
abuse our relationship otherwise the
indignations will keep us further away than
we kan ever imagine of being/having a notion
of a viable available nation once again that
is based on mutual love and appreciation
rather than bitterness that reigns so that
familiar desire we useta have for one anutha
caint return and cling to our hungry spirits
that kan only be properly fed by us if we butt
use the keys that nigga Solomon even tole us
about that unlocks the cock block of the
magick inside all niggaz which is able to
help be the glue to hold our relationships
together in a very intuitive way because one
thang about us is that we know how to do the

impossible with nothing and miracles mite
take longer butt we know how to perform em in
untaught ways to slay cuz ours is a natural
art of the way of the heart which we must
follow back since it knows the way to have the
black man and woman standing yet again once
more besides one anutha in old fighting mode
that useta whup untold ass and took names
later of all haters and procrastinators n
pretenders n wannabe contenders hoo tryna
slow up the party that was going to the break
of dawn cuz a real nigga revolutionary party
dont stop in an insipid shallow world led by
vainglorious crackkkaz hoo must be addressed
in the sternest possible methods without
kindness weakness or diplomacy due to being
under the rong impression that the enemy is
cordial enuff for reasonable talks realizing
not that he is wickedly inclined and always
ready to scrape to prevent the escape of
commonsense upon discourse when approached
thus cruelty being his steelo is brought in
exceedingly hard upon niggaz heads cuz we
keep making that same mistake that allows our
kingdom to be torn down n overturned with
fatalities of our peeple since much of what we
go thru with racist whitey n other evil
ethnicities that side wit them outta
ignorance is due to us becumming transfixed
by false omens which allows our foes to bend
us to their will and seal the deal of our fate
for dates with no end in sight the victim once
again of anutha mans hostilities n lack of
moralities. And this be the type a shit that
keep us outta each others beds ya digg
without a constancy of love lovemaking n
forsaking the bullshit that would seek to
pull us apart because when the black man and

woman exist at that level we kan stave off the werstest shit the werld has to offer no matter the long drawn out day or nite or fright or never mind how weary we would git we had that thang where we was like stars in the sky forever shining and refusing to drop no matter the severity of the critics or killers of spirit or body for in our superior forms death was easy if it came to that because there was gone be a whole bunch of the muthafuckin enemy that we were gonna take with us to the grave and if they didnt kill us we would be back between the sheets in dat meat n greet fucking in such a way that portals n shit be opening to brang a nigga sum more juice courtesy of a boost by the ancestors waiting on the other side with pride that their progeny was doing the damn thang to death to preserve life inspite of the strife cuz thats how plugged in we were that we were able to snatch victory out the jaws of defeat since we knew how the trick was done with the Crackkka mans gods we didnt need or heed cuz we had taken that shit to a whole nutha sacred bold threshold to behold. So that being where we gotta ascend back home to since we let ourselves be excluded frum the perennial rule of the black dick n pussy across the land that we busted many nuts on before the sertain kkkinda white man showed up with his sheetful ass talkin outta both sides of his mouf or sobbing n trembling like he aint know and needed help and us being the kinda muthafuckaz hoo always willing to help anutha fell for the hideous villains okey doke and every since the lesson has been wretched and harsh in our faces as we descended frum our thrones being

condescended on in this land of our homes
with moans cuz the shit was gone and damn
near not even knowing no mo who we are or
where we truly frum yet be that we are living
in an atomic age full of certain type of
molecules of cool that stir up the
bloodstream of those of us with that ready
melanin the change and the chance has cum for
niggaz thru a new form of bonded love to
climb the heights again and return with
retribution using the old stile becuz
supremacy-minded whitey surely caint stand
ancient tactics that fuck wit his snynapticks
frum niggaz hoo now know how to live in
opposition of the status quo of the foes of
warring attitudes. Butt let this be of
cognition in recognition that we are more
skillful beloved to blend our shit 2gether as
black men and women niggaz n niggresses and
achieve our natural progresses n functions at
this junction as we go back towards the
perfection of our black whole souls which is
where our ultimate happiness rests in that we
forge an avenue for provisions of our
decisions for our successors in a manner that
they be better lovers of one anutha than we
have been able to be to one anutha and so
perform their duties to be that nation that we
hoo live now shood have been which is why i
am diligent bout publishing the kinda truths
that have not only been hidden in plain sight
with great pains so it wood not be discovered
n killed butt it has been forsaken by others
hoo mite know it yet here i am revealing its
rotten core willing to burst the bubble of
trubble that has enraptured niggaz
imagination and not because im more daring
wit this sharing butt because by this stage of

mah life on this page of mah life i have no
fear ya hear of a discordant government hoo
wishes my precise demise as an exercise of its
mere function as an evil defectiveness
covered up by aggressive bullying and mirage
of triage that to this day remains n maintains
their effectiveness in denying the black man
n woman frum resolidifying their union so we
are mutinous with each other instead of
libidinous with each-um-other which wood be
a much more preferable predeliction of their
jurisdiction of our relationship as well as a
riteous refutation of wanton white supremacy
thinking—wich does not make it so- yet its
reputation   for   vulgar   definition   n
destruction   of   our   shit   just   on   pure
ideologickal principles of war and the
thangs that follow/flow frum it which we
know is the degenerative self hate that
destroys niggaz noble affectation one for
anutha putting us outta position to git into
possession of ruling ourselves as a nation of
fortunate future. Butt since i have never
presumed to accept the obliteration of mah
peeples   existence   under   such   grafted
reprehensible pretenses as to despair and
give up the ghost as despair leads to
nuthingness and i am too much endowed wit
the nigga power to act to doubt mah self or the
universal magick at mah aid since i know how
to tap in against the vicious vile sinful
atheistic attitudes of the enemy hoo see
themselves as sovereign masters of niggaz and
act as such to the point we agree it is so that
it is up til now where due to the changes in
the werld me n i know other real niggaz out
there are now kwik n ready for retaliatory
violence and dissolution of the customs

habits n actions of amerikkka that has heretofore rendered us essentially effeminate without a backbone in many respecks in their presence butt no longer are we wanting to maintain an ordinary stance or presence of being afraid because they appear to have all the weapons to kill us cause they dont as appearances are deceiving as they are meant to be when a show of force is presented often when a bully has nuthing to show in actuality butt is only huffing puffing out his concave chest to induce fear in muthafuckaz hoo dont know no better bee dat they have gotten afraid so this is how they set up their institutions that they send niggaz to for brainwashing and sloshing ineptitude so we will live running scared instead of awared of laws and a god that doesnt even exist cuz he aint real except in our imaginations ordered by them since it was created in their image yet their war machine bizness is merely adorned with a lotta bells n whistles that mean absolutely zero as a true sinister necessity that mah peeple need to respeck as an infinite danger butt more wit disdain as we realize we been had under madness and demonic hostility for a lifetime of lifetimes moaning wounded among huemanity frum the trickeries sacrifices drawn frum depths of depraved knowledge via the enemyies coffers that have been stolen pillaged over the years n used as revenge on us. However it cum to this day n age where niggaz such as i are ready to draw down the moon if we have to wit reckless abandon yet strategic scorn to overcum errors that led to terrorization on us cuz we didnt heed the proper warnings of agonies that have been visited upon us as familiar prophecy that surely all races must go thru when they neglect the intuitive survivalist instructive scriptures of their niggacestor ancestors. Cuz Brothaz an Sistaz are ret to depart frum suffering at the hands of the enmity of the enemy by cumming back to roosting inside real love that be that authentic amore shit that sustains a peeple when its as genuine as its sposed to be that many talk about butt dont know about the art and discipline and how when its done rite it fits you like a glove to rule like tailored clothes befitting u having u suited zooted n booted so perfectly that it alone scares n terrifies yo haters and those hoo wanna cum against u due to the magick poppin off you so they caint stand only wither in the face of real love as it condemns them to a bitter mournful hell of grief and garbling for their shrunken shriveled frames to the point where they will wanna die instead of remain but death wont cum to the bums as they cry in anguish that the endless nights of gloom caint be extinguished on their false faces now living a cruel reality they deserve as nature wich also abhors the bullshit avenges wounds exacted upon niggaz previously fallen to new record lows cuz we got caught up in the throes woes n blows of the powers that be doing shit in the werld. This is to let it be known so that it is renowned before its all over that niggaz is officially off the chain loose reins and sumbody done left the gate open and we rushing to return to a lustful state that werked as war when we was doing it properly in alinement wit korreck magick metaphysikal forces touching us in the minds how we need to be stimulated in order to be triggered to shoot our shots of love for each other and hate for the diabolikal ones cuz understand how the precise distribution emotion is to keep ya love inside you and ya hate in front of u when dealing wit the wild beasts of this babylonian empire in their attire n accoutrements of stone cold indignations insults and injuries to common peeple as long as they are willing to putt up wit lowdown laws instead of taking to the streets or ethers and upsetting this muthafucka where necessary to bury the fools hoo keep this insanity going n sowing seeds of horrific acts into society so they cum off as the new normal instead of the abnormal sickness it is that being what it is it still aint too late for us to play it back n deliver payback on a level never seen before in this modern era since the ancient of days n ways of the warrior gene that resides inside melanated ones so before curfew we return to virtue and even better if this position i have taken wit werds be fodder for the fight to brang shit to lite n our foes to ruination for their past heinous deeds for they will have no answer for our nouveau new world order assertive aggressive untaught guerillaish war ways of dealing wit them in battle for we are destined to revenge our own selves due to those of our peeple hoo have gone on before us doubling back across the great divide of death frum life to assist us for having gone astray off the familiar path as royal original heads of the werld rather than being seen as merciless ignoble savages who are useless beasts of the field taking up space n co-existing in places of criminal lifestiles because we are an undistinguished vermin festering reproducing like cockroaches in hoods across amerikkka which is a description mainly becuz niggaz refuse to conform to that barbarous impolite white kkkulture deems honorable tho they have no honor among themselves. What they most fear is no longer a guess of mines butt a divine knowing for truly i was born not just knowing but born understanding as well yet have often gotten away frum my birthright a result that punished me appropriately altho as i was saying their fear is our reconnecting as black men n wommin in love supreme and missionary zeal so that we are back to writing poems songs n letters about emotions long gone that we cut ourselves off frum that used to be the glue that held us together me and u forever u kno hooo when all we had to live for was each otha without material bondage and the trappings of civilization to poison our hearts and minds wit ambition while deepening attrition starved us both of lack of feelings butt no mo as this apocalyptic age closes in on us branging the moment of denouement the vizion on the horizon up to the vanishing point sees brothaz and sistaz approaching one anothers arms again to be embraced in bountiful passion like it was when we were igniting the world strickly thru fucking all nite long in various positions exuding semen in vaginas that were making half on a baby for a whole lotta cum uppance cuz we couldnt stay away frum each other due to black power solidarity that wasnt a rarity then like it is now yet changing as i speek these werds to paper as we reappear again to one another as star crossed

lovers ready to tongue and sigh between
thighs n caress phalluses n ease calluses &
explode wit passions dat been on hold n was
reserved for fairytales not real life but this
is that life for real to heal the rift and
empty loins so we kan git going n sweat
tremble n heat up again frum sustained bouts
of sexual healing on lumpy mattresses we
break in as we drank up each um otha as we
lose ourselves as we caint help ourselves
falling back krazy in love wit ourselves so we
kan use hate not just love as a weapon on the
various vulgarous villanous vandals hoo
once held us down like gravity but now we are
set to ascend as firewerks go off frum bouts of
erotic courses of intercourse that exhausts
our totally dazed senses filled wit each
others torrent of sayings utterances and
incantations of forgiveness as the urge to
purge riteously continues to sweep over and
thru what we do to our clinging bodies
slipping hands into soft spots engaged as we
are in super ghetto sutra for that super type
of sexual transmutation long known to be
remedial alchemy for defeating enemies and
staving off misfortune when we cum back into
the bed riteously in a way that shapes stirred
deep love into an invincible fortress of
defense against venomous hurled epithets
meant to instigate divide n conquer us
however winds up not being able to do
anything butt be a lame lamentation or a mere
symptom of a failed attempt to mount an attack
frum a deluded sick mind that will only be
able to watch helplessly as niggaz scatter
their shit upon the hatred of their wishes.
Far be it frum us to delay copulating in
accord wit the hood sutras of old that when we

were on point were used by all like minds to be of a regulating commandment passed down tween niggaz to be used tween leggs by us all to treat our co-existence wit respeck and we were a wonderful strength hoo served at length to the werld needing examples of black love harmony and togetherness so that we never clashed in any way and none especially of the known enemies cood cum between or amongst us to split us apart for we had earth on lock frum crackkkaz hoo in many respecks is not even of this werld so he kan produce no visible effects to affect us when we are rite n tite in the eyes of black man to black woman which is due to us speeking proper game at each other and being conversant in that shit of knowing what werds go where cuz being and somethingness caused in us an inflammation of eros that was at such a vibe we knew how to tribe n conversate one to anutha so that shit happened when ever we fucked or blended between the sheets and there was those hoo wanted this never to happen hoo didnt know how we were able to do so much werk in the bedrooms of niggadom or how we were able to acquire knowledge not found anywhere else by stroking butt they didnt understand and perhaps shall never overstand that when the black woman knows how to katch the black mans stroke then the protection of what is acquired becums desired n all butt guranteed in the niggakashic records where every thang is written to be passed down thru korreck game or sexual mingling n tingling due to the proper method of action when niggaz are on the same freakquency moreso for black wommin because fucking on time wit korreck riddims secures their lives as well as the bag sumpen that the brute creation known as haters of niggaz caint komprehend nor indulge in to stop for his pleasure because he gits off on inflicting pain for gain to those he views as less in his perspective which is failing to intuit that niggaz werk frum a sertainty of possession rather than the doubt of obtaining a thang definitely in regards to what life has to offer of her own free will that u caint steal unless u know how to feel which the crackkka mind does not to a large degree and therefore violates the ordinances of respecking anutha mans shit thus payback being what it is has seen fit that we have cum back to sexual konnection that is the foundation n groundation of the beginning substance of a new life since we know fucking in the rite and tite way is the prime mover of all thangs that need to be moved under the precise guidelines of brownian motion that govern movement in accordance wit the laws of nature that were in place when we got heah butt then sumhow and sumplace when the white man came upon us in his way that he does shit we got away frum the tenets that had heretofore kept us in it and on top because being riteously structured highly favored and set apart niggaz knew how to git shit done n seemingly miraculously accomplished without us even have to break a sweat and its to be this type a gitting down thats going to be the thang that reinstates us back where we belong again as per our destiny. Eye more than any thang want it to be made clear that mah offenses against the black woman are to be forgiven for many a time i knew not what i did and i want these werds to be seen as an apologetic elegy of a mournful period for

that life i lived that disrespected mah
wommin and even mah own mama at times when i
became apopletic due to the programming i as
well fell up under that permeates niggaz
minds at times so that now here in what
amounts to six decades already since mah
birth near the same orbit at which i was born
initially it has been made gloriously evident
to mah mental how i erred wit the wommin of
mah race so that i beg of yall to see this
moment as mah attempt to save face n brang
salve to a situation of mah past fucked up
alliances n dalliances with the pussy proper
wich happens when one has cycles of wavering
and thus adheres to an antagonistic doctrine
that pits one against what one needs to be
wholly for instead of halved in two and cum
against ones self even yet ignorance does
this to a man and he becums a resource without
recourse and puts a mans life in perverse
reverse instead of where it belongs wit his
woman at his side full of pride and divinity
into an infinity of purposeful protest that
gits results because we are no longer werking
on stoopid gumptions of assumptions about
liberty nor werking on mere ideals of freedom
written on a worthless paper called contracts
that bear content not meant for hueman
consumption only presumption designed to be
a beautiful koncept butt its reality is
pregnant wit the most severe punishment the
enemy kan putt on us. I having recognized
much of what has gone on in society have
recovered mah nature as a man like me must
since mah kind are seldom met wit in this
milieu so by now the changes i have gone thru
have shown me that colonizing korrupters
have been the evil that has influenced mah

peeple to that precipice where we deigned n
fell in piece by piecemeal including mah self
butt this misstep makes me rejoice that tho i
derive no comfort frum mah derelictions of
duty in the past i have finally recuperated
just in time for kontinuation of this
dispensatory discord wit a renewed
conviction and so this narratory was
necessary because im not ashamed of the many
times i have fallen shawt in fack im more
happy n nappy that you are here wit me in
these actual werds of stirred knowledge as i
arrive back to mah self in terms of
consciousness to perpetrate these revelatory
troofs designed n aligned to brang down the
enemy frum whence he/she/they/them of all
pronouns have stood for a good long time upon
the necks of mah peeple butt now we got next
baby against the evil that men do n have done
and won so far as they are koncerned butt in
their zeal failed to realize the degree of
gitback that cood be brought back n about
frum the prodigies amongst us hoo respeck
truth as a capable agent of reckoning and has
no peer among equals butt instead points out
constantly insufficiency where it is present
in plain view or hidden in plain sight such
is its purview in righting what was long rong
and branging just due back to memory back to
reality wich is rooted in ancient highly
favored muthafuckaz hoo have borne all good
will and an assurance towards us niggaz left
to exist today to deal wit destroying
amerikkkaz shit. Therefore subtle reasoning
is no longer an option if we are to dispose of
the commodity of hate and conspicuous
unenlightened crimes against us committed by
men hoo used ingenious ways and means to

snare our souls so that we lost all cognizance
of what goes on not only globally n federally
butt locally contributing to our oblivion
even in the eyes of each other of what was and
what wasnt or what is and what aint & what
gone bee as the case may be or not be is the
statement of position we have dared not
respond to over the years and so have
permitted the punishment we only later came
to abhor butt without understanding our own
strength had becum the whores for such
existence and those hoo read this hoo account
themselves mah peeples may be offended yet i
caint in good faith not say what has been said
thus far and even that which will be said n
read after for it has fallen to me at least as
far as i kan tell to be dat nigga hoose level of
indignancy is such that i must spit this fiery
game without werry of its offensive nature to
those of ERRY RACE regardless of COLOR dat be
the enemy hoo are of a sensitive being as life
has taught me that those hoo are often
offended the most are the most atrocious
offenders of life itself so that mah natural
inclinations to speek truth to power cowers
those contemners in many respecks and dulls
the ground they walk on frum even just
peeping this incriminative cummunication
that i was most obligated to write in witness
of the unfavorable nonglorious treatment
mine eyes have seen as a party to the real
nigga race hoo wherever we are oppressed via
ignorance malice or violence then that
society is poorly furnished. Especially
regards how it keeps Niggaz frum that
original stage of love we must engage
harmonize in and is as explicable for breath
is to any living or breathing thing to be

forever viable not clashing as liveable beings for it is only real love that as it repudiates evil also regulates devils how we copulate n congress wit each other and make worldly attainments rule royally in the kinds of union that places us within the proper dimensions of desire time amusement n protection when war is our only option to secure our lives and property and magick cums to our aid frum within our bodies where it naturally resides inside as dormant forces n choices of action becuz it is that ingredient which will always arise within us when we are man and woman 2gether in the appropriate observed coda we are unstoppable untoppable peeple against whom lies have no currency and falsehoods are humbled crumbled into lowly matters of unimportant magnitude where they caint be used to exploit us any more since we know how to fuck our enemies outta existence n persistence even resistance as seeds are planted in wombs to yield crops of new niggaz as the rebellious fruit of our loins that be lions ready to exert notoriously upon the heads of those foes horrible foibles hoo object to our return to form and so seek to harm and make us a victim of scorn wit empty loquacious arguments as they have always done followed quickly by the unriteous rumors and propaganda that normally brangs us down into a mess of distress and destruction where we are despised by all hoo believe those hoo operate at a low nature rather than the subtil spiritual nature of niggaz hoo simply dont want no trubble and thus often quell our voices instead of obtaining argument fisticuffs or violent maneuvers resulting in death of the prevaricator as shood happen to any or all hoo sully an honorable name reputation or character without just cause. Fortunately it was always written that this moment sumone like me wood be dropping a missive such as this to became legendary legacy immediately upon reception reading n absorption into consciousness to be a trigger that black love nigga magick is back baby and feared as niggaz cum back to it wit moans faints strokes that fits us as the uniforms of soulful souljahs soldiering n mounting noble stallions racing back to bedrooms to press thighs to thighs as we no longer denies ourselves conversations we shooda had long time ago as melanic gods touching hands feeling vibes mending hearts talking that shit that wooda kept us frum departing one anutha back then since we are the ultimate perfection of each others whole soul butt let slip away cause we had lost the ability to know how to hold tenderness which is a butterfly that inherently rests upon beauty only and when or where none exists it flaps its wings to keep it mooving n grooving to the next properly amorous episode so that it kan receive every thang it deserves frum that moment instead of being as we were wich was so defective we were not just void of love butt even without memory or knowledge almost of ever having the habit of making love. Butt this moment in which we now live has brought back that first thirst we once had for each other that had been quenched as like water we return to rise to that previous level of worship not warship for the other that had us tasting the sweetness in the other for bitterness couldnt exist then nor cood

dispute of action that wood brang on weeping
sounds n unfortunate hollering since brothas
n sistaz knew better than to bear false
witness in our bitness or allow expressive
werds destined to kill the spirit into our
innergies in such a harsh manner as that
which wood be unbecumming to kings and
queens holding that type a stature such as we
were holding at that time and have now
returned to at this dire timeframe of the game
wit new capabilities n precise korrections
girding our loins against perpetual highly
konceptual attacks frum haters wishing to
stop our mutual great passions wit their
uncensored commentary that mite as well be a
sin against us turned into punishment and
exile in order to cause us to be cast out for
dubious reasons especially in the minds of
those hoo believe the enemy tongue is valid
in making us accountable n perennially
fallible unjustly tho it be in reality yet in
the eyes of the gullible they accuse us of
causing wounds to society so that when the
diabolical claim we are the problem the
following poverty that visits upon us is
thought to be deserved by manipulated
imaginations hoo cant see our god form only
cheap esteem diminished by liars hoo practice
telling the truth to them hoo be easily swayed
by embellishments against commonsense that a
good reputation has gone bad because such is
the amplification of error supplied by the
fiends it gits transmitted as authentic
alignment and the discord which was the goal
of the evil mind gits affirmed the more in the
conscience of the naive receivers hoo becume
the perceivers of niggaz as infamous
stereotypes hoo are seen as tripe n less

worthy of generosity by all races of the world
hoo by a certain time and constant listening
to the evilarchy about us regard our own
werds in defense of ourselves as mere hearsay
that they dont wanna hear us say because
their senses have been so dulled to reason
that the goodness of hoo we be can not be
ordained as realness nor penetrate into the
interior of their inner ear or minds and
strike their faculties as anythang more than
just a blemish that we are simply trying to
diminish instead of seeing us as being
genuine articles that evil players wanna stop
the prophecy frum being fulfilled that has
cum to spread itself to the many and the few as
it is written because those hoo try to stop it
must be smitten since as i must add it is
fitting that the pure werks that keep the
world frum collapsing in upon itself is
destined to cum thru niggaz in alinement wit
the venacular of their dna prime directive
crystal structures wherein which rests our
ultimate happiness and perfection of the soul
we forsook due to deprivation that in turn
kept us frum our riteful place in the
universe. We are together now and the one
mind that we are as man and woman is a wedded
welded n melded knowledge no longer
handicapped by where we live and have
meaning in our natal hoods which for 90% of
niggaz tends to be outta the environment of
how loftily crackaz teach themselves as
opposed to how lowly they teach ourselves
which is far removed from the truth of
knowledge of self told as a defeck they love to
infeck us wit so that we leave behind
liberally whom we really are and go thirsting
after a told fairy tale never to be found or

abundantly understood so that we wood wake up if it was taught riteously without shade butt since it aint we wind up eating the meat of obfuscation and that becums our level of intelligence built upon racist biased knowledge they buy us that we claim as our own thinking since now the crackkka mind is in our nigga mind frum that moment on and our consciousness is easily swayed and played more often than not in war with one anutha wich is to be expected when you are taught to behave speak act without virtue by sum other race of peeple hoo have no luv for you and yours so they make it their bizness to keep u on the threshold of extinction level events without an ability to galvanize yo peeple for revolution or resistance in a timely manner cuz the brainwashing run so deep most of us sleep. Butt when you are a nigga like me born and bred and sent heah wit a higher nature at this particular dispensation wit dat incisive information because its at a time when mah public teachings n reachings kan be at their apex to hit korreck in the mind n sinews of mah peeple and be stamped upon their synapses without lapses as we prepare to collect on a debt owed us by posterity thats long been in arrears for eras behind niggaz tears frum past generations yet thangs being what they are were meant to change and they have and so we cum forth for that ass in this harvesting rather than worshipping season thats ready to yield as it must to the real bloods hoo had to slack back in disgust while the hueman artificials took up residence via offense on the thrones once owned by shunned niggaz like me hoo have returned like the prodigal

son after much difficulty to undertake this
even more difficult task of spitting this game
to the hearts minds bodies n souls of those of
you ready to receive the sustenance rolling
off mah tongue cuz i aint tripping in a way
that upbraideth mah niggaz becuz i kno no
other way to deliver a regenerative radikal
rebuke raw call to war which is just as much a
physikal battle as it is a war of werds n ideas
and yes ideals n ideologies that must fight
the odds n the ides in this final push for
empirean status where we belong as part of
our paradise that is our claim that was borne
of us as first peeples hoo had birth upon
earth in the beginning when it was void and
without the white supremacy-thinking mind n
poisoned traitorous hearts of other races it
was only us as tenants wit a oracular strain
of tenets locked in our bosoms where they
cood always enrich n guide our steps for the
well being of the werld as we evolved thru
life as royal heads of this kingdom cum joint.
For the process of running the werld was
always meant for the least of the races
according to the holistic sagastic scriptures
that forever function as the total capacity
that predetermine the engagement between
gods and their sons and men and their
daughters and the potentiality of all
relationships between peeple who must becum
actualized thru pleasurable peaceful means
and werds spoken in agreeable tones without
maliced forced thought or phony politricks
so that we not live under oppressive
discomfort which has foreverly brought
infallible ruin n total dystopia desolation
to the races of the earth whereby peeple learn
to live wit and be comfortable wit

abnormality of spiritual emptiness
becumming the zombies of the apocalypse and
lying consciousnesses and hearts be aching
for lack of authentical muthafuckaz to speek
to the issues at hand being as they are
overruled by zealous capriciousness that has
the most effect on the hoi polloi all in an
attempt to keep me and mah kind frum exacting
revenge upon all mah enemies and frenemies
since they know im heah to tax korruptive
doings n ruin without reflection only
korrection n reset the balance is mah goal
using whatever it takes by any means
necessary even wit bile risen in mah
liver/jaundice in mah eyes/blood ret to be on
mah hands to exorcise the ruling party of
these demoniacs maniacs wit as forceful and
just as evil a purpose as was used by them to
alleviate niggaz of their former royal
positions frum on high to wretchedness drawn
as we were into condemnation to increase the
wickedness in the werld cuz we got lost n
turned out by game by a type of reprobated
mankind and a kind of man we were not used to
dealing wit so this correspondence is written
in an urgent manner against whole swarms of
insurgents hoo must be at all costs
exterminated n exorcised if we are to finally
cum frum under their plague of pimping
purposes that have been etched so deeply into
our minds full of crackkka brained trained
essence wit an inability to see ourselves in
dominion and of our own opinion thus we
basically cood only act like fools shifting
shuffling and as a farcical trope of a dope n
as dog and as a roach on a leash as ours became
the story of the cuckcolded negroids of
disgrace living in a nassy place swept along

by mental collapses of the synapses dumbed
down by merciless media enchantment of the
fourth estate into our lower estate where we
rate less than the usual detritus of a
foregone society due to much of our core real
niggology being lost thru the injuries of
time frum the unjust causes that nevertheless
brought the disastrous effecks of a shipwreck
now cumming home to port like chickens
cumming home to roost becuz our progenitors
await us knowing that we are more than the
mere trifles we have always been taken for
being seen as inferior beings fit for nothing
more than to grovel or graze in the field as
slaves hoo behave as knaves when the truth is
such positions we cood never embody in
honesty cuz they are foreign to us altho
natural to the enemy of gods hoo traffick in
such actions as normal to the werld in wich
they live as stealers of flesh almost as pure
religious zeal. For theirs is a reasoning that
finds its discipline in the practice of
sorceric scientifik research that imprisons
tortures n maims the seemingly disobedient
hoo they also kill and string up by their
teefess after they confess as public example
that their politikal cartel must be and betta
be adhered to as law since they are not
rational beings tho they seem created by the
same hidden hand frum the same land this wood
be an understanding that one must disgorge
oneself frum thinking that there is relation
cuz surely it is unreasonable for one to do so
i must make this articulation clear forever
in these writings that no further injury
befalls a nigga is why i spit this game to make
it thoroughly rite in yo mind of what time it
really is and whats really goings ons in terms

of niggaz at last being benefitted and cumplimented and redressed frum the secretive meanderings n maneuverings of the sinful ilk hereby being constantly exposed werd for werd so u knows dear nigga frum first to last the imbalance that has taken place frum one ethnick group n their allies frum otha ethnick troops to anutha in these conjectures being made publick to clear shit up about a lotta purloined points in the past so take what im saying as extreme exactness against all the wackness n magical sources of prejudice that plagued us using combinations of strange change n mores to effeck an end to their vile villanous means wich pushed their ungracious weight on us to tilt the scales in their favor as one of their best contrivances to stacking the odds n rigging the game of life which is how we were terminated frum royal title n separated into korrupted blood and thus deported frum being in position to git into possession of all that was our inheritance not by law butt by birth on earth first inasmuch as we are the original aboriginees of the hoods of amerikkka meant to have great influence and therefore i presume those of u hoo read this are ready to torch the inerrant learning that lodged in yo mind by the enemy and moove forward into the intelligence of yo inner divine nigga figga where it will find a home lodged in yo bosom tho be it despised frum a distance by mean fisted eyes looking to always distort the character of a whole race of real niggaz. Yet thats why its being expressed so fervently by me since i know the destiny of its value as part of our disorderly crusade be made so that we violate all their laws into abolishment by

cutting out their barbarous customs as tools
of tormentation upon us therefore me having
refused to be compromised all mah life tho
full of mistakes that i beg pardon for mah
days of repugnance n ignobleness when i was
without proper character and ears to hear
thus was often a source of mah sorrows that
cost me dearly before I woke the fuck up butt i
say this not so to seek praise or love and mah
motive for these notes remains without
exaggeration thru out to press the advantage
that time has highly favored us wit as
recompense to the historical response of
debauchery and delirium that we brang it to a
disastrous end as catastrophe is sertain a
remedy for the shituation at hand that has
hitherto failed to yield to sweet
conciliatory compromise we sought in the
company of them hoo have been our foes frum
the very beginning once they came frum
whence they sprung and we became the lynched
n hung in the terrordome. Nevertheless truth
and justice are ready to be received becuz the
first time they were upon the earth they were
disrespected whereas truth was pressed down
and justice was knocked down & killed
efficaciously n wretchedly as possible under
sanction butt truth didnt stay down n justice
has been resurrected for the mean souls dat
must be dealt wit post haste wit da most hate
necessary for our renewed assault on the
content putt in place by the new werld order
as cum forward wit divine providence as
evidence we are touched wit a new mark of the
best rather than the beast for we are no
longer held in ignorance to mysteries that
defiled our dignities and divided our souls
frum our bodies while we were yet walking

round in em thus being executed by such tyranny heaped into our headspace that depopulated our mouts so dat we lost incisive cummunication sound rite reasoning one to anutha wherever we formed loose cyphers. Butt as i said not now tho as this discourse on karma is a bitch n payback is a muthafucka waiting to be reborn in sync to be insolent to form an embed in yo mind even be a vision before u within yo selves so down deep in u that even yo skeleton is aware of operation whup ass passing into thought without diversion or perversion as we are so unbridled n unriddled this day n so willingly to turn up to show out to commit even death to the grave. Thus its a must dat our advancement is at hand in such a way its meant to be inconvenient to the crackkkaz wit pure intent in it for us to win it at all costs since we are now calling bullshit and judgement into the werld onto the flesh of those of our foes in fact of all races not just the racist alabaster albino fools none of whom have integrity filling inside them to nourish them or inform a better society instead they chew up n spit out class n wound niggaz heels in a bitch of a brutal fashion to the ungrateful extreme in line wit how they run government wit every lewd breath they take forever which is a form of necromancy that they love so that not just peeple butt places exist as dead n wrangled. Therefore I speek so u have no doubt of what i say this day of reprieve to git eve without artifice or said anutha way shit is real as the trickery has run its course to secession wit its writs warrants arrests codes ordinances n judicial hoemongering cuz true woke consciousness is

summa the most severest revenge to the
muthafuckin end dat u ever wanna sees no
matter the pleas or please it caint be
deceived only received in the spirit in which
it is meted out to a muthafucka hoo be the
venomous hoo deserve it & more of where it
came frum for we are forever out of patience
this instant not tomorrow butt now in lite of
the thousands upon thousands of
racially-poisoned peeples of all ethnicities
in all cities wit their cock-eyed motives
retty to do bodily harm to the sorry lot among
us butt this time we kno our counsel is sound
and our advice is full of the exact passion n
interest to disperse the wicked back to thru
the wormhole caves where many of them
originated frum and the rest will shift n
shuffle along to their place that they will
find and git in it when we instigate riteous
action for a return to the throne whereupon
there will be further interruptions of our
beaucoup bucolic legacy which is what
almighty shood happen when revolution
restores proper reverence for those of us hoo
remain in this day and have awakened wit rite
memory of the scriptures big mama nem passed
down to us indeed left within us so we cood
whip ya n do just whats bout to go down in
fack its going down as i spit this shit
wherever niggaz be n kan cum across it wich i
know they will becuz nuthing kan stop a nigga
whose time has cum to stop being troubled by
the spectacle of the guilty especially when in
possession of the korreck supreme
mathematics n divine utterances rather than
the gross mistakes of yesteryear that had us
in fear like a deer caught in headlites wit
fright so we cood not fight. However that was

then this is now a proclamation affirmation n declaration of a return to the living nation without the feat of self conceit or deceit so dat we be mo apt to avoid hereticism that has befallen so many werld nations befo us that such significance has not been lost upon us or escaped personal purview that is our solemn intent leading to meaning and value as never before in ourstory on earth as it is in heaven which has always been held within we the peeple left behind hoo have formed posterity and now prepare to delete conservative miserableality since we be the future generations talked about in the holy book of niggamaste which says seek ye first the niggadom and all thangs will be added unto you and all real niggaz after dat becuz we stay on dat divine mission of attrition and refuse to fall back on the old propagandistic ways that held us sway much of it because we gave silent agreement to despots without reproof korrection or enuff vigor n lost our spots n instead we held back and virtually acquired set backs of the falsehoods that fractured our beings and forced onto us an adulation of our undoing which we now throw off to reintroduce into the peeple our niggaz a type of liberation theology thinking that was once thought impossible under the perennial regime of gross degradation and ignorance that many of seemed to have made a solemn oath to so aint no way i whudden gone cum forth at sum point and express publickly mah calculated international sentiments which i stand on as i *spitestament* to mah willingness to give mah life for onliest the realest niggaz bunched up and ret to go when the werd is given which these werds here on this paper is breaking a long held silence against violence and meant to trigger to kill burn or destroy whatever needs to be killed burned or destroyed to throw off the yoke of tyranny as part of the great werk we must do especially involving foregoing being sensible in the face of the nonsensicalness eternal recurrence animosities and prejudices that have always haunted our existence on earth butt no longer as the union of love between the black man and woman is nigh so as to end this awful amiss shit. We be them able advocates today ready to rise wit a holy zeal of perfeck offense to go beyond evening the score against amerikkka whose lady liberty is a spiteful betraying bitch hoo took off her chains and putt em on niggaz hoo were yearning to breave free n kalled it a gift that continued as a present of cruel indelible wrongs n injuries as tho thats all we were good for and no moreso than that and yes as i have said many of our peeple succumbed to the terrordom and the brutal opposition to our souls and thus were discouraged yet this new path we on frum niggaz like me the werld over spitting fiery new visions are a revengeful reminder that deliverance is here and in our own hands outta the hands of the man so those of u hoo read these werds i look to u to amplify the power of them all over the known lie and even hidden werld so that they figger into being the restitution reparation for our sovereign nature for these werds have been resting in mah contemplation for an eternity and now match mah conviction to spread their utility as a protest to blind submission which heretofore has reigned wit undisputed persuasion over the mind of the nigga. However whether we niggaz know it or not we have no choice butt to ascend due to the prophecy in our blood that even tho amerikkka be theirs amerika shall be ours that has been written as well in the stars not just our sinew butt first we had to be krucified and our essence made to run as rain as a large portion of our lives passed while we did naught according to the purpose we shood have been doing thus those wit false names have ruled constantly n nonstop causing us to die daily as a normal part of living when we shood not have been looking forward to it instead we shood have been checking the desires n ambitions of those mankind hoo had a mean birth and grew into a harsh nature yet were never able to be curbed or putt into check or balance therefore our own divine cyphers decayed into ruins however this moment we hold destiny in our hands along wit the winds of change that previously were so fleeting they slipped away helped along by our denial of what must have been done butt we didnt adhere to first principles therefore of course what i say now is cognizant of all that has gone before so i hope u feel the infusion of mah warring spirit corroborating this discourse of action encouraging you to embrace rules of engagement as foremost and as new habits of dealing wit our enemies for we have multiplied to the point of whereby we kan now force our customs to becum visible everywhere even if this must be done thru a matter of bloodshed which at this juncture is the most expedient route other than conversations n letters already tried n failed as a means to peaceful remedy for the liberty of mah peeple butt those cunning peeple were not trying to hear what was being said by the likes of us and kept on looking only for disadvantages to exploit among us as a way to continue governing our behavior to their benefit so we have nuthing left to say at this point in time butt must prepare to bring the pain and as needs be violent factious ferocity as only real niggaz kan do to affect greater means because we must increase while our foolish foes decrease since this is pure unadulterated scripture troof about winning back our natural born honor that was ever a wholesome portion of virtue among us that we let enter into horrible disgrace n becum an occupied country of peeple hoo had lost our special ordination due to such a general error that led us into believing we had been conquered wich in actuality was butt a highly pernicious delusion that kept us in a subjugated defeated state of mind such was tyranny n disorder n cunning created in the community frum those depraved minds and that was the beginning of the pains n sufferings which of course were often veiled in korruption wit the power they had to keep the black man n woman sexually isolated and in ugly total outrage rejection of natural practices against ones will leading to what cood only happen under such circumstances that of disastrous ends. However that has expired in the current milieu at this singular endearing express werk that im confident will remain indeed it must remain as a monument n a treatise to the scourge upon the whole werld that crackkkaz hoo were born

of delirious fanaticism and frum wich we
stand to be delivered as the moment is at hand
and outta the hands of those hoo once held us
in abeyance rather than obeisance thru
pulling   us   in   so   many   directions
simultaneously thereby hastening a downfall
into   self   destruction   that   wit   no
exaggeration on mah part caused untold
deaths. So u see wit burning affection for all
of u mah peeple we are living in a time for
glorious increase of our magnificence into
an   even   higher   amplification   befitting
niggods per respeck of our beings viberating
in resonant absolute truth wich has never
differed frum prophecy nor will it ever be
inconsiderate of the whole truth that was set
down in our bloody hearts til we assumed the
form for it to be fulfilled then too i had to be
in the rite place at the rite time to present
what im saying at the level of spit required
to penetrate the ethers and hit just at such
the rite angle that souls wood be delivered
frum mental slavery and moove toward eternal
reward as triggered by this whole werk that
the enemy will see simply as a rant a screed
deed of a vulgar tongue whereas u the
initiated will see and inhale this as proper
prosaic votive diction yet one that is not
subtle about its investigation of amerikkkas
shenanigans inclusive of its derelict morals
n ethicks which are long overdue for being
destroyed by us using causative powers at
willful deliberation without reasonable
conscious interfering to upset the balance of
the frequencies that await alinement as we
advance knowing we have nuthing to dread
frum these last evil trifling players nor do
we hafta to be afflicted wit guilt by those

whose fate was determined the moment they
defiled the prophets it was for them to be
conquered in time of which they have been
uneasy about erry since for they knew as well
yet sought to hold it back butt that which is
preordained yields always to the conformity
of what must be so that possession to the rite
muthafuckaz becums automatic restitution
remedied by the universe that we all find
ourselves organically within dealing wit
original sin. Despite this i dont count on
overwhelming konsideration frum the many
only the few for mah passionate thawts and yet
i would be prolly be alarmed if not sad if
these werds found agreement within the bosom
of ERRY BODY so no i dont expect nor want the
ingredients that make up the content of this
skroll to be to erry bodys taste nor do i
wanna feed the masses of the asses whom have
ever been the used up and unfortunates when
one seeks to do so in an attempt to curry favor
wit as many peeple as possible and thus
despoil ones self plus go into madness
therefore i understand that this is for the
needy not the greedy hoo are not afraid of the
rigor of unhinged vengeance. I have
fashioned mah werds so that nuthing is left to
chance or guessing of mah ill intentions for
i dont want there to be any dout that a
revolutionary mindset was in the midst of
niggaz thinking at a time when they most
needed butt failed to heed it if it cums to the
level of contemplation that sees abandonment
of the ideas laid down heah against the
opposition due to timidity n credulity and
fear of offending those of a sertain white
gaze hoo built fictions into their diction in
their minds thus their moral order is

confused wit no real konception so it allows the werst of men to reign rather than perish as they shood wich if this be the case i kno no amount of attempt at shaming will make one wit of difference for such wretches in mah own race hoo have succumbed n now werk wit the supremacy minded mentality thus they will never see their sublime rongness in this present day as being in the way of intelligent response to the shituation at hand that has becum a well oiled automaton machine of deleterious repute that few are willing to dispute wit as much bitterness as i am born to do since i was never meant to be useless against such low moral antagonistic evil becuz by nature mah faculty for reasoning thru difficulty has always been superior to those hoo have cum against or that i have been sent to reproof conclusively for i am fortuitous in that respeck. And therefore where there wood be difficulty for the average muthafucka for me mah effort is compensated by the infinite strength granted me so that i will not ever have to concede reasoning or ground to detestable probabilities presented by the adversary as proofs when they are really of an ignoramus quality and or purely fallacious tho bodacious they may be in appearance or imagination i will still yet be able to see wit the help of the niggods within how their falsehoods are taken for truth by the gullible because they dont know how to be investigated carefully or thoroughly and be a touchstone of legitimate provenance towards being revealed to be able to be copasetic. Of course I kno sum will see me as a fool n such will be mah posterity and of this i have no

werries for what is a man if he does not do or
die not just try wich by itself is not enuff if
i am to be rated a fool for daring to cum up
against the status quo and be seen as having
an immense defect of intellectual capacity or
may be the record will show that this was all
a hazardous biggie type-a-dream that brought
me unnecessary danger n consequences when i
cood have done as most negroes and relaxed
mah self n slowed mah roll n jes been in a
quiet sanctuary of agreement wit the enemy of
mah peeples while remaining a lame skeptic
rather than risk dying an undocumented
martyr no one will kare bout when its all said
n done and even mah ashes will be
disrespected when i am no more perhaps at the
hands of the evilarchy hoo will convince me
before they kill me that I have wasted mah
time and that im too late cuz the prophecy has
expired and that im no visionary hoo has made
a dent in the foundation of the seductive
diabolikal rulership and that no peeple has
sent me cuz its a figment of mah disturbed
imaginative mind and that i am only meant to
suffer a furious privileged authorized
destructive execution for i am no legitimate
heir to power as i think i am nah i am but a
seditious nigga hoo must be putt down like a
rabid dawg or putt to the chair where liters
of federally funded n authorized poison kan
run thru mah cauterized veins n kill me after
the needle goes in mah skin for insulting the
limits of the current leaders. Thus they will
commit to a meeting to discuss how best to
persecute me and mah goons for being at war
wit them n their coons for wickedness against
their truth according to them in an attempt
to astonish us wit their brutal dictates n

mandates wich of course will not moove us to serprize at all bout these serpents for we already came into this especially mah self wit eyes wide open knowing the sore score even before the game began understanding there were surely to be no compliments for a job well done only a singular determination by the perverse to suppress spirit if not outrite murder those of us taking a stand against The Man & His Minions of the same racialized opinion. Nevertheless we not only welcum persecution we honor execution if need be by the violators of human dignity since that is their forte of fostering delusions and opening chasms in peeples peaceful coexistence thereby imposing their will on the summoned n submitted without embarrassment even being composed to speek evil as tho its mere sugar coated powdered language to motivate when its really meant to torture injure or mutilate psyches to an extent that draws blood or causes mud floods n reduces the affected to fragments beneath its profane assault becuz they have been left wit no refuge and to make matters worst the whole werld blames the victims hoo are without ability to argue their circumstances as they have happened and even if they try to the system is rigged for maximum vig so that they will only sound as tho they are the one wit the fabrication in their commercial legalized speek before the crowds in the counterfeit courts of amerikkka. As such nothing will ever be prooved and what u think are facts are simply apparitions appearing as real thus they are mutilated n struck down by the judges without enlightenment warmth feeling and definitely without logick whereas in these places of law evidence of ignorance outweighs cogent meditation on proper application of rhetorick meaning that all yo well planned werds are frivolous n never meritorious under rules of their unvivilized procedures n legal maneuvers thus they will continue to say i am a blasphemer not a redeemer that i am a fruit masquerading as a vegetable n this will be part of how they tax mah flesh by the pound by saying thangs that only have authenticism under the aegis of their psychosis psychoanalytic epileptic conniptic religious system wherein they will accuse me of attacking their gods n douting their infamous oracles and prooving their prodigies to be pseudo intellectuals. And so of course for this i am a repugnant smell to their noses and so of course they are easily persuaded to dead mah ideas afta they have read mah ideas MAYBE & proceed to shut mah mout frum saying i sed aint important cuz they kno i know their distinctive routines frum all the thousand of lives i have lived in service of bangin n branging a proportionate amount of whup ass erry time i show up again in mah newest form as an incarnate being of divinity wit mah mind full of a essence of volume of insites as defense and offence for their korrupt asses. Cuz erry time i cum back i cum back wit a mission to banish them wit mannish illmatic ill-mannered strategems based on magickal even geometrickal tactics they aint never seen afore. Thus they find it hard to handle the collected malice issuing frum mah fingertips n lipps altho they are known to me frum centuries of doing this that i too will suffer as it must be yet i count

victory as mineses/failures as pluses and
despite difficulties and long hesitations
balance will dip into mah favor baby since
once the veil meant to reveal their final
destination has been lifted nuthing kan or
will stop the original intentions of the
nigga ancestors whose shoulders i stand upon
so that i wood be able to take advantage of
weaknesses in the affairs of the many
barbarous leaders of the highest distinction
in the hidingest places hoo have led this
werld to shame n shambles to be a wasteland
dismantled frum the inside as is the custom of
those hoo corral/steal freedom as those
Negroes are such stoopid beings they dont
deserve it so its popular to bleeve we cant
exist without being ruled and betta not be
left to the designs of our own divine minds.
Thus we need governing accordingly for let it
be known that governments are not
established for the good of man butt for the
sake of laws that wielded as the weapon to
make man good where he wood otherwize be
badd without such ya digg?? Please
unnerstand that at great risk to mah self n
those brave enuff to bide wit me in a
turnabout is fair play nee revenge piece i
nevertheless can not fail to write what must
be written n sed altho what will be sed n may
sho nuff reach yo ears is that dat will b
described as being of scurrioulous
superfluous rumors manipulated to deny me
gallantry in yo eyes if not for ever or even a
shawt time the efforts of mah enemy will be
increased on mah behalf to make me a
tragickal figger of ruin and to magnify me as
mere spectacle hoo was always brewing to be a
catastrophe. Butt i ask u to ask yo self what

truth is there really in the lies of the racist alabaster disaster terrorists kkkind hoose kontrol i announce to renounce wich to kno me is to know that i ignore the rules of any man that ever was born lived n died upon earth and im saying this all at once for i have no assurance that every thang i say will reach u yet it is mah eternal hope that quite a few of the werds of this dismissive missive especially the cogent salient points will find their way to yo hearts n minds n encourage u to join me in brotha n sistahood because im counting on the bromide that says such hoodness preserves goodness of unity due to similarity and for that reason i wish mah werds/verbs n syllables to be werthy of yo eminence that i have never taken for granted since i kno yo attentiveness for wich i thirst cood be dependent on sumthing else in anutha relationship pulling you in a different direction thereby casting mah shit aside to unsertainty if not downrite destruction. Yet this is the presumptive chance i had to take that u wood be disinterested in mah flow to git mo and Y not since i kno dat men even ignore their own gods frum time to time. Furthermore i also innerstand that many are not given to cognize that moment when its high time to confront errors of eviltry irregardless of the black fack that i have made mah bestest effort to show u how its been given to me to kno whats up wit lousy muthafuckaz hoo have denied our peeple respeck for our beings n divine freedom sumthing bout wich a nigga like me cood in no wise n in mah own eyes remain silent as nite in amplification of the same without the whole being tole instead of half stepping. So please dont mistake this as the ravings of a lunatic mind as they will point me out to be butt intake the whole cake of what im saying wich is the simple yet involved premise of this werk regards a barbarous peeple without souls whose morals n ethics have comprised not just a theory of destruction butt an equation of life n death. In other werds all that i say here is revelation butt not merely so just to be exposition butt to be as well an invocation and a chant to brang down babylon frum inside out as these werds are expressed within yo chest as witness into the mouts of devils hoo have fashioned such an immoral werld government built up to make us oppressed sufferers of innumerable seasons of unjustified charges for no reason under the sun. To wit i kno mah own safety is not an assured thang nor is mah rep due to be without severe haterade since i am exposed as i lodge this information against the opposition i fully expect sanctuary to be eaten up by mah accusers no matter if i was innocent or not for innocence is without rigor n only condemnation is a foregone conclusion. Butt i dont care not one iota or omicron bout their snares n have no interest in admitting rong doing in their kkkounterfeit kkkourts shood i be dragged before the black robed magistrate really a white hooded raconteur for a rape of justice hoo wood feign to wanna set the record strate butt only produce evidence to find me guilty of treason without reason so this is mah transactional translation of the what had really happened free of forgery n falsity. However as i said we know blurred perceptions rule crackkkaz contemplation of

matters n never will an innocent nigga travel
freely to find enslaved justice under their
gavel wich seeks always to contrive villanies
to unravel & convict a nigga whose only sin
is his consciousness was stained wit
drapetomania that is to say merely a mighty
mental desire to be free of tryanny terror n
torture n not necessarily in that order. Butt
forever on orders of the diabolikals whereby
wind of such thinking that gits back to them
is punishable as a sacrilegious act cuz that
kinda meditation upon freedom is seen as
becoming a god as they see themselves wich is
totally forbidden as an atrocity against
their rulership as well as a rejection of the
established quo teaching quotient that are
their ways n therefore deserving of sum
wicked designated dishonorable undignified
fatal brutality. Nonetheless U hoose eyes are
open to read n ears to hear what i say here
peep the remedy in this deep spit bout this
real shit much of wich came to me in rem sleep
cuz u and i kno the shit fits erry bit as a
curing of obstinate sickness if u let it join
yo spirit for alliance rather than kontinue
to be in the realm of the illusion of monsters
for hoose image n stile i came to ruin that i
may brang u back to unparalleled splendor as
u git rid of the calamitous splinter in yo
mind so that it vanishes surely if not swiftly
upon proper receipt of this game orchestrated
to lift you outta shame and the grief of false
beliefs and even more incompleteness that has
so long hinged upon yo lack of possession
that you felt impossible because a nigga such
as mah self had not cum giving u back to yo
self so u wood not want anybody else.
Wherefore now i present u wit an opportunity

to be yo own master in the castle of the self that as such is obtained in korreck alinement is not a transitory thang sum one kan easily take away outta yo possession thereby rising u above all hoo refuse to acknowledge their inner nigga figga for fear of trifling retribution frum cowards masquerading as brave men when they are knave men full of inherent impurities that are positively no accident of nature wich is always precise in its application of capture in the ingredients pertaining to the substance wich make us hoo we be for our intended end. So in this wise its accurate to say their ill will is not the service of a friend butt a force of inappropriate relationship to make one a servant hoo submits n obeys for neverending days without proper unnerstanding to a beholdened massa. Yet niggaz like me remain always a problem for the charismatic charlatans due to mah natural nobility self sovereignty n incorruptible spirit that was fashioned in line wit mah daddy n mama bloodline based on resistance long before i got heah butt was preserved in the nut that mah daddy busted wit the necessary expedient ingredients that wood sustain me lnce i got heah to deal wit pale-faced knowing that thangs wood cum to this just as they are as i write this compelling tome to brang u back home n telling u to take a close look at these lousy muthafuckaz hoo have lorded their shit over us for hundreds of years butt now their obsolescence is heah to dry yo tears. Thus such asinine rulership is consequently extinguished and be it known that we niggaz have no affilation or association wit them and in fack must contradict all parts of the

whole without stuttering for the masters
nature is not ours and never was meant to fit
us perfectly as if we were sposed to wear his
bidding willingly as part of the kin of our
skin & no matter that it was disagreeable to a
nigga inner being like when we are tole we
cum heah wit a sin based on a god they give us
that has no resemblance to us butt
nevertheless we are sposed to harmonize wit
his rules of said commanding virtues that are
really propositions of pure vice dat aint
nice wich yet n still by its beautiful
persuasive chicanery caused so many of us to
depart n digress frum long held sacred
practices that held us 2getha forever n
thereby obliterated our established real
nigga ways/ya digg?? And much of what has
kept us away frum ourselves has been the rule
rather than the exception until mah time came
as it is now. As a result im shooting mah shot
wit this fiery commentary i speek at u as i
have been mooved to defend mah peeple
meaning u you and especially you frum
disparagement and bullshit so that yall may
be brought back to truth under the lite of me
having examined their intentions of
hundreds of years pass n revealing their
defecks malice inappropriateness of their
construction wit what is being said heah that
it be of a confounding expression even
inconspicuous to the muthafuckaz as part of
mah attack on such perpetual contemptible
destestable disgraces that they are. Cuz its
high time tide that we be free of them so peep
mah discernment in ditching their fake
opinions that others hoo came before that
were sposed to be like me butt were instead
false prophets hoo had or let their minds be

distracted n directed away frum the mission
by statecraft witchcraft because they were
not authentic at any rate n just mere excuses
for real niggaz wit an empty desire for glory
thus their baseness of mind proved they were
never ready for the close-up kinda enemy we
face today wich just goes to show u that
pretentiousness makes a man measure himself
greater than the wretch he actually is
promoting wich is a contender when he is just
a worthless pretender to the throne.
Therefore when questioned by authenticity
they kan never answer in the affirmative
without exhibiting the ridicule that resides
within them intrinsically butt does not
belong to them since its only inherent inside
real nigga figgaz whose genesis is not frum
here meaning the fake can not be exonerated
or explicated by a non existent alibi that
they dont have because otherwize those such
as i require no real proof since hoo i be is
self evident even frum the beginning of mah
life this has been acknowledged wit no hard
effort on mah part cuz frum the start i was
meant to be sent/ya digg?? Whereby mah
familiarity as the true prophet is sealed and
guaranteed frum time immemorial for the
gathering that sits upon us as new light n sun
ready to shake the darkness away so we kan
have it indeed as we ought to have it as it was
always meant to be haved. So wit this in
sublime mind n consciousness i implore u to
understand these writings as fighting
weapons instruments tools stones
reinforcements let loose n made available at
last as counterattack to counteract previous
devises of the enemies vices that tho they be
crafty maybe even ingenious their defense be

drafty in addition they are not wonderfully
made butt are the types of men hoo scorn life
for this is their fateful mishap that the plot
of the lot of them wither since what has been
ordained kan not be averted nor diverted for
the perverted that they are and steady being
yet saying that they are a peeple like us
rather than the unstable imitation they be
that has failed to adapt due to their
inculcated hostile sickly beastly thoughts
wich constantly n subsequently consequently
makes them set to be a predatorial mob of
permanent danger hoo by this time in our
existence we know they are not gonna change
their repellant desires to be attractive to
earth instead seeking only to scorch it and us
wile we try to hold fast to riteousness like
fools in the face of these greater fools hoo we
must avoid and withdraw frum or else no
matter the cost and i say this wit so much
force not to u the many butt to u the few and
to u the audience of one hoo have yet read
this wherever u may be hoo are ready to derive
benefit for this contributory pact of
transformation information bout the sick men
hoo inhabit this werld that is our home. And
irregardless of mah unworthiness in summa
yall eyes including the tyrants hoo have
skeduled all of humanity for exterminative
calamity in their myriad ways and so no dout
will position this piece as puffery n empty
phrases of a stile dear to politrickkkians
rhetoricians n the like and so mah desire is
that this most spleenic jeremiad finds
considerable acceptance wit n be diligently
read by the rite ones baby hoo have been
wishing to overcum obstakles they have long
had to confront as they stood blunt n

defiantly fast without consenting to the
jurisdiction of our opponents fist no matter
how much he has rattled like a snake and
threatened danger n attempted to draw blood u
rite ones have been bold and refused to fold
frum the challenges so for u i must offer u a
solid. Cuz u are cut frum that fabrick they
dont make any more nor is the mold around
anymo that they made yalls kind frum hoo be
determined to resist the power of evil in this
hour for you are the type of proof that future
n rite now niggaz need to see in action
rejecting fear n factions frum yo face as u
throw it back in unparalleled abandon frum
whence it came frum the bowels of the
opposition hoo wanted to frighten u into a
witless state of uncontrollable panic butt u
wood not collapse. Thus its for u i kontinue
to write becuz u are substantiated in mah
book as to the present premonition of these
conditions of decisions that must be made wit
nary any apprehensions between you wich i
kan feel on a vibe level and therefore i kan
tell that yall along wit me will survive any
executive violations that brang executioners
our way wit a song to terminate us. Yet they
will find us oh so astute n resolute wit all
the elements in our favor because we be them
sons and suns of fervor/unafraid of
unsertainties or willing to settle for
moderation instead we want extreme justice
knowing we have not only niggacestors on our
side butt natural born talent abilties gifts n
skills that came heah wit us as price TAGS of
our bonafide sertified value to the werld
that is our fortification against ritual
abusive fornication used by the diabolikal
oligarchs to block their demise at our thrown

hands for by this point we have been wise to how to protect ourselves frum the unordinary beastiary that is them without falling to terrifying coercion or any of their retinue of contrivances always in use since they crave bloodshed on erry head and displeasure to all those they feel are beneath them unfortunately for them its too late becuz their time ascendancy along wit dat ass is up forever whereas the riteousness ones that be we special breed of real niggaz have broken loose frum the chains that they cherished that once held us mentally not just physikally. However lemme say this to you in particular hoo may sho nuff be feeling what im saying wit gusto in this manifesto of passionate call for real muthafuckaz hoo are fed up n retty to go heads up for all u are werth/cuz if i kno u well/and i feel i do/u are the kind like me hoo knows that things that the enemy thinks are pre determined and therefore can not possibly be changed kan in truth be changed indeed altho they mite be forestalled or even caught up for a minute on sum irksome bullshit to fool the publick nevertheless i kno yo spirit will not lose its impulse to avenge all that shit that needs to be avenged n revenged. Because we are the ones whose hatred of dastardliness knows no boundaries or limitations when its time to git even steven thus we stay ready so we dont gotta git ready to hand out punishment n suffering to such a degree that we curry no favor to our foes we bury our foes toes deep to settle indebtedness owed to a nation of niggaz for any thang less wood not be the demonstration of truth that must be levied upon many of the white mind of warring thawt and their multiple ethnick comrade allies as they are also known for all the havoc n shock they have wrecked on humanity turning it into zoomanity in taking all liberties yet the turning of the tables have turned for the further dismantling of their crumbling dire amerikkan empire as it did wit rome greece n china hoo felt they wood never fall butt no one is beyond their evil receiving the commonsense of recompense no matter how dense the degeneracy be. And mind u if u think this rap is too long or superfluous lemme remind u by pulling yo coattail even harder to the game i spit cuz shit has gone on too long without the proper judgement wich had white supremacy-minded fools feeling like their shit dont stank butt see the smell of shit lingers even if u cover it up in a spray of tranquility like every thang be kool wich is really the motivations of an attitude of madness in denial of actual facks that he has been headed for self destruction of its own accord since the end has been cumming approaching wit the greatest weight of gravity and invevitability wit no chance of reprieve the moment they manifested it wit the error of their ways and werse refused to have it pointed out to thim as pathological behavior. Butt instead of heeding this as warning chose to take it as a threat of a weak peeple simply using a pretext to steal back what they had stolen by any means necessary sumthing they thawt died wit a previous prophet. Butt now that real meaning has cognized in their brains its too late for diplomatic counseling to stop the rebuke they thawt was a fluke that real niggaz are preparing to heap upon their heads as hot coals in accordance wit vows we all took to uphold the greatest good of a purpose driven life free of the crackaz gaze n ways and directing our steps n taking credik for our thinking frum day one while we marched n protested which is now over as we are fully realized niggaz wit overstanding that power wont concede not a damn thang without an ass whupping if we want niggadom back on earth. Thus those of u hoo hear me i have no dout are peeping the game of reasoning that i have unfolded since im emboldened by time n circumstances to stand against men hoo must be stood against irregardless of whether the many hoo may indeed be among yall hoo think im being non sensible without even innerstanding mah flow butt they dont kno dat this shit is happening according to a grand plan of alinement and ornament that they are ignant to cuz their comprehension be slow to to mah flow of werds that have preceded or mah werds that have succeeded thus far as follow up to this point as indication of their deafness and true understanding loves to conceal itself frum fools hoo have no bizness peeping meaning in the first place of mah raging mout that spits rude and unadorned utterings for bold codes n signs that will always remain difficult for those hoo aint got the rite ears to hear or hoo aint proper enuff to be accessible witnesses to mah niggamonious testimony. Therefore mah knowledge shall stay invisible unseen n opaque to sertain of yall since yall be those hoo are unsuitable for mah emanations based in seeds of cosmic origins and all dat they contain/ya digg? Furthermo becuz what i drop heah is for the righteous among u only all

others will maintain an unfulfilled craving
for misbehaving boundaries to disperse their
know nuthingness just to keep truth obscure
to souls hoo need revolutionary doctrine
most yet u types are prophesied to keep access
frum this pure adequate form of manifested
niggaisdom wizdom grown heah in these pages
wich brangs insites to the polemics that
punish us unto death or introduces a belief
in us that we are inferior or too primitive in
the werst way. Tho that be far frum the troof n
proof and is only said cuz they caint decipher
mah shit n say its too strange to brang bout
change in the status quo that has existed for
years due to fears butt the indestructible
present is heah exit it now baby/ yaheahme!!
And no race has ever been mo ready for the
werld cum up than us niggaz down to the least
of us hoo have had to deal wit cruel
annihilation passed down as repetitive
tradition that we were sposed to welcum as a
desirable friend courtesy n complimentary of
amerikkkan diplomacy wich is a smile in yo
face stab u in the back regulatory act to kill
n punish muthafuckaz hoo resist their greeks
bearing gifts attempts to pluck out life for
the acceptance. Hitherto shit is not
explained herein cuz u hoo have good god
sense also have the consciousness the masses
of asses dont n hoo i aint tryna communicate
wit no how as a necessity of these principles
that needed to be imbibed n encoded in order
that u flee the werld dominatrix hate tricks
of this matrix asap poste haste wit mah werds
in yo ears as a meaningful guide butt
incomprehensible bitter extreme riddles to
ane fool not meant for higher heights outta
the deeper depths of mah bowels wich is now

71

no longer a secret anger held within to do me
harm cuz i thawt out rather than bought or
sold out the brunt of mah assertions in this
flow that i had to be obedient to in a
ceaseless war for a nigga sanity for we aint
just the salt of the earth or the ashes of the
dust we are the hope of the werld whose mere
inkling of thinking is the lever that moves
gaia irregardless of where we stand in
archimedean pose posted up so the lite among
u will see mah shit as contribution despite
the tribulation or reputation of mah
nigganess preceding me or following me as
threatening shadow while the obtuse of u hoo
exist to assist mah detractors n enemies will
be disturbed to seek mah destruction as one
hoo is an abomination insane in the membrane
when the precision of mah write mind has all
along been to free niggaz imagination frum
rongful illicit worship of falsely validated
illegally created crafted freaks passed off as
genuine gods replete wit miraculous powers
as weapons used to kill u when u sin or
stumble over their commandments cuz u moove
ya lipps when u read em. Butt mah vision does
not want dat 4 u for i am blind to the ways
that wood deny mah peeple liberation even as
i am willing to accept the pains n penalties
if that be so much a part of mah destiny for
that wich i want for u me n we has infiltrated
the crevices of mah being so deeply i am now
irrevocably committed to altering the course
of his story for our story wit a violent effort
if need be. And shurely i have long known this
about mah self that i discovered in mah in
borne resistance i was meant to disappoint
the plurality of negroes especially those of u
hoo wanted to live comfortably in delusion as

tho not a dam thang is rong wit dat as an example to the rest of the gullibles hoo caint see the real for the fake folly of an imaginary contented fantasy they dont want disrupted by the application of higher technology of divine intuition implication wich tends to invade mirages and wake peeple up frum being hostages to counterfeit dreams and if they have any sense at all will be convicted if not they will go the way of all flesh that deserves to be rent frum the bones as if vultures were picking at the meat. So i kare not that u see mah tone heah as savage sayings cuz they are definitely not an apology to man thus summa u may respond that i only feel this way becuz of mah own failure to understand dat niggaz were bred to serve sertain slave-oriented whiteys in the midst of living and that mah determination to abolish their falsehoods crude magnificence & cheap shots is premature n askew in the cycle of time despite that the prevailing crackkka race n unkle samboes among our own peeples have done nothing but shed rage blood n death at will via dark powers n ever newer forms of tyranny without being overthrown. Thus n therefore there is nuthing too down n dirty that i wood not doo to conquer these demons gone unchecked hoo be issuing catastrophe while being a disease to all of huemanity including this explosive exposition that will be heard if not read cuz i already kno what i have written down will be passed down carefully as a loaded weapon amongst u to the rite u and if not now during mah life they will be used sooner than later to deliver retribution n revenge for mah real enemies in whatever way that shall be fitting the walking dead including slashing burning decapitating gutting beheading slaughter of entire families if need be as we be gluttons for vengeance. Yet the age has changed so that what i say that u r reading i kno stands a chance of vitriolic censorship frum the powers that be dat hate me following mah instincts and intuitions that have fallen trippingly off mah lipps as werds that are even confusing to mah self butt this is as it shood be as part of the riddle to keep the rong ones in the dark as i am just a conduit for what is cumming thru me. And even if i have to write subsequently in a penitentiary to git out mo of this truth be that as it may be necessary after this then so be it for i wont change mah spit frum the street to the boardroom suite in the face of these degenerate punks to fit their ideal of a model well behaved slave. So no i have gone insensitive and will kontinue to act like i aint got no muthafuckin sense i was born wit as long as im fighting these rude souls hoo have not a trace of of whole or even partial unnerstanding bout how to deal wit a nigga like me cumming wit rite knowledge to be a reliable witness to what these beasts of the field have done over thousands of years much of wich tho it be unknowable is felt nonetheless in the psyches of niggaz thus affected hoo submit to a revolting revulsive repulsive compulsive regime cumming apart at the seams and it seems that i be the son of those real niggaz left behind to be a fiend and a mighty presence to their rain of evil dat lets them reign n gain a function using savage sophistry against the peeple thats no fun for we the peeple u wanna keep pressed

down wit policies that keep us in a headlock
or u want us to drank the koolaid or hemlock
while u act sacrosanct yet have no moral code
fo real. Butt since in mah mission i owe
allegiance to mah niggaz of earth i was built
and sent to stay in constant dissent of
societys arbiters even if i be condemned wich
shurely is not a guess or promise butt i kno fo
sho to be a guarantee yet i kare not for that
is not an observation for me to be koncerned
bout i only kno dat i was bound to write this
gory story to tell a tale that must be tole wit
mah whole awakened mind to a sleeping werld
& lying rabid dogs hoo have dogged mah
existence wit the izm of dogmatism.
Nevertheless i have never been afraid or
scaid of going into battle against mah known
n unknown adversaries wit mah total entire
being for as long as it takes or til the end of
never wich ever cums first as dealing wit
vicious peeple kan take awile sumpen im not
adverse to if this effort be a protracted
endeavor wich it may well be as i said as i
strive to treat mah foes as they have treated
me and mines to wit to give as good as i have
begotten and never have forgotten such ill
usage that is shurely enuff justification for
mah hellafied attitude in response. Tho i kno
what they wanted frum me was respeck due to
fear an emotion i dispossessed frum mah ego
quite sum time ago as i knew it wood not serve
me well in mah orchestrated git back for
slayback that blazed up in me like a fever so
that i knew what the magnitude of cure had to
be and such brought me sleepless nights since
i was now triggered n activated by a dormant
responsibility that had been prefiggered n
placed into me at konception for this

korrection and cood no longer be hidden
under or forbidden by restraint. This is Y
speaking these werds were mah recourse to
action to undergird the stark realization of
the faction of mah ogre opponents n mah
peeple kan rarely be friends and such is the
case between the racist crackkka and i and
mah peeple that history has substantiated as
unhealable consequently as i have said
repeatedly and it bears repeating this
invective it is not without cause butt for
good reasons that us niggaz seek our proper
place in the pantheon of held space without
policy written by those wit the blood of mah
peeple on their hands that is an untolerable
situation in due course of course so our
opposition must be laid to a big sleep
necessarily in lite of our new intentions
manifesting themselves as determined
declaration that must be seen thru until the
powerful all fall as part of our vehement
wishes as we mend all of our own case without
waiting for crackkkaz scandalous attritious
eyeballing to recognize us as viable virtuous
muthafuckaz hoo deserve to be great.
Especially since what i am kalling for in
this drop is a result of thawts that no longer
have reverence for a despot government
masquerading as a beneficial platonian
republic cuz we have passed on frum that
type-a-shit seeing as we see that the estate
must be overthrown asap. That is to say
REMOOVED by foul demand n reasonable or not
becuz rebellion is natural to throw off
oppressive dictatorship by the unworthy hoo
devour us up as a commodity that is traded as
an oddity on the open global market and while
they feed on us we starve in our stomacks wit

discontentment dat ironically they see as contentment if not overabundance and then this gits tole as a tale of truthful statistics of a racist algoriddim built for sale in a capitalistic system. This is why baked into mah werds are no room for apologies for the brunt of their content for they are real whereas before they had only been imagined til mah courage forged of its own compelled by a desire to be free and unfettered frum foreign alien arrogance n abuse of power and i wanted to be unceased frum. Therewith nuthing in this document shood be seen as boasting mebbe roasting or toasting butt not braggadocio nah its mo obsession n the possession that has stoked me to a high desirous discontentment to kill off racists n traitorous coons holt on niggaz gentle self expression so we sink no further into misery frum their rank n power wich korrupts absolutely for most and if nature hates this shood not niggaz whose spirits are incompatible wit such stank behavior that will forever be incongruous wit dignity. Yet they hoo wield the sword love the effeck of branging peeple to a conclusion dat includes death be it mental or physikal to scorch them as earth as part of their daily slaughter full of laughter that being their steelo as ones hoo have no intrinsic worthiness that amounts to such scant real value they dont deserve to even have habitation wit real humanity because their amplitude for violence n barbarism rather than civilization only spreads without virtue across all boundaries n fucks all different diversities to a level of pain they as enemies never refrain frum only go towards at errry turn of the screw so that any hope of splendid glory is limited to the peeple since they only want for us oblivion and anyone wit any superlative conscience they want wiped out altogether to nuthing doing but ruin. So that environment endures endlessly as prison however i be dam wile i yet have breath will i standby and not wage eternal recurring deceitful elemental fundamental warfare n nevermind if mah face is revealed cuz im gonna remain implacable baby ya digg and will steady be fat badd moufing erry time i find werds to make clear mah thawts such as in this drop of slop thru the cruel gruel odious adversities mentioned heah against wich i realize i must never cease warring as a naturally implanted nigga figga hoo is back on the attack for the reattainment of dignity for the highest nigga good frum those previous errors dat fouled our aim to prevent their skemes meant to drain us n lead us astray butt in the end we kno now it has all been a false show full of rabbit tricks yet it aint no fun when the rabbit has the gun to shoot down the iniquity of the wicked fools allowing life as we know to return to proper proportionate function all over the werld. Because thats when we will see a perfeck disappearance of capricious contamination n contempt in a most efficacious manner that is to say that murder and mayhem must cum frum those hoo have long been under the thumbs of these bums hoo rioted our lives n diminished our beings as a plague on all our houses for ever even down thru genes as an epigenetic curse talked about so that we actually helped harm the true nobility of ourselves. Butt trust n bleeve when i tell u that at this very moment of the werld we live in the beasts are uneasy wit the crown on their heads that belongs to us the once past servants future kings of now time as we are those hoo were prophesied to cum frum the fleshly nuts of the old niggaz of antiquity to stop the ubiquity of their iniquity in a comely timely manner so that their serious evils that follows them erry where they go perish in a plot writ long ago due to our renewed solidity n swift motion that will pierce thru any and all obstructions as offense they konsider a form of protection. Especially since they have always been nothing but wretched mortals previous butt misled niggaz saw as gods of renown so rather than branging em down we faltered as mentally enslaved prized possessions of a kingdom of the vilest thangs. However thats over as i set forth to manifest not just a new werld order butt a nigga werld order nourished on the real roots of nigga resistance that kan and will last n survive generations of haterations no matter the feces any species throw as various forms of shade or no matter how severe we will endure becuz by standing on proper ground we will resist disintegration of our souls this time around plus our remodeled self love fashioned as it is outta authentic niggaship wont yield easily to divide n conquer wich has always been the standard to destroy us as fast as possible. Because of course a lotta the reason for this was self hate was deeply rooted in our consciousness to the point that we were crippled manacled by these architects of the evilarchy thus they reigned n flourished butt we niggaz have at last reached a revolutionary conclusion of exclusion that def is not one of inclusion of crackkkaz disturbing actions becuz our will this day n shurely mah own is about gitting even instead of asking to git even that racist tighty whitey kalls gradual equality wich has always been an empty statement if ever there was one. Therefore i am he sent to stimulate those niggaz among u hoo are ready for the reckoning that is to say we be those wit a natural revenge that is consequence for bad rulers in throwing them outta power as good health rectifies a diseased body and is a sign that proper order n balance is being restored for we bout to labor for the rarity of a victory for posterity. And so those hoo wonder or ask outrite why am i hoo be half authentic prophet all real nigga be the chosen one for this i kan only say that truly the nature of the beast made it necessary that i be born to it to do it in order that future niggaz cumming afer me be enriched therefore i had no choice in the matter not that i wooda wanted one butt to have done otherwize wooda dam sho putt me in arrears of mah duty and wooda effectively assassinated mah character via a self inflicted wound. Of course i knew not to let that happen because mah desire to brang a certain kkkinda white man to his predicated end grew in me as that thang in me was realized n ordained in me wit the distinct foresight of function & mah own gumption to perform in this realm thus this was the differentiating characteristic in me that made sho i wood follow the presence of mah essence and as such this competency was mines alone above all other niggaz hoo had their roles to play too butt this was mines for this existence and is limited to real niggaz of mah particular divine bloodline never to be reduced in meaning or potentiality nor capacity to handle all primal primordial matters also known as thats how shit gits one n done so that we as niggaz kan be self realized individuals rising to our highest nigga good as we shood in hoods across amerikkka as well as round the werld where sum ever we are in the aggregate to congregate so u see i was determined to git down to expound on this shit so mah spit is utmost testament of a flavored fervor directed at the expected end of white-minded supremacy as a legacy per the formula embedded in our DNA aka divine nigga attributes that is tried n true in resolving all thangs that must be resolved n revolted wit the precise provocation thus this is why mah werds have been a constant repetition that their empire must fall like jerichos wall so that we may live ritely again wit sufficiency proficiency n efficiency as well as deelishisly as part of the great tranquility that will sweep over us when their shit lapses into ruin pursuant to our dooing what the fuck we posed to be dooing wich is standing on infallible troof n proof for at this point the crackkka rule has stunk for eons as unrighteousness peons yet has arrived at a place it kan not exceed wit any amount of speed nor proceed forward to a reasonable end since they only kno disagreeable behavior wherefore they are no mo supreme not that they ever was butt this was a teaching many of our kind believed and received to be true thus we suffered as superstitions of this kind kan often be very powerful n effective in faking niggaz out hook line n sinker as a result of falling for the rope-a-dope of hope shit the diabolikal one employ and thus they gain the permission of submission of way too many of us in the past butt this day that ass is about to cum to its singular end as the day prophesied that included me cumming back to give you to yo self so u wont want nobody else is heah. In other werds i hoo be hoo i be will draw so close to mah REAL niggaz that mah skrimf that be frum the niggods will pass to those of u ret to putt in this werk to despoil their perversions on the way to yo conversion n turning out this brute beast so we all head back to niggod positions. I am heah to expose their true wicked natures their true hidden form their polluted minds their cruel crimes their disguised motives their pedophilic ways their evil emotions their false premises their terrible theologies their unjust inflictions their pitiless predilections n punishments as i follow in the footsteps of the shoeprints laid down for me that is the blueprint for apprehending all parts movements n motors of whites wit racist attitudes using an apparatus kalled government to maneuver mentals n coerce compliance to mandates. Henceforth i and we caint be stopped since our minds are ruled by sum brand new flavorful shit so that our purpose will be fulfilled under a new jurisdictional process that will carry itself to infinity under niggaz once again to be indispensable to the universe becuz what is ritely ordered can not be rongly disordered when its peeple are in alinement wit knowing that whiteness is an abstract and has no real rulership value no where in the known or unknown multi dimensions except programmed illusion as their will is undone for nuthing kan remain inimical to a bunch of niggaz on board wit one accord and therefore must terminate in our collective presence thus u must go forward wit mah werds digested in yo belly because the chosen among u have eaten of them properly and now they are in yo mind too and has freed yo steel will as propositions of certain logic so that u kan never again be hindered in any way since this shit i drop is the type-a-slop that has what u have always needed yet never got its influence to drag u away frum the persusasive substance of the friendnemy and the foe alike using politricks that encouraged loyalty under false pretenses butt for this i had to be the one to show them unapproved because there be a white belief and even a coon betrayal that is evil butt it aint always self evident to muthafuckaz so u need anutha real muthafucka such as i am to expose the hoes they be. Thus let it be understood that mah hour has cum to drop this game to all mah real niggaz hoo are ready to be guided by me so thats why i am the detergent sunt to be used to clean this shit up frum the ground up for those hoo ready to deliver that check up frum the neck up to these prejudicial bastards n bitch asses of all creeds n colors for it aint just me dooing or talking its a part of our prophetik story speeking thru me for an operative conclusion that will be so valid so thoro that the likes that has never been seen before and may well never be seen after. So mah niggaz i shall end by saying this: i have never grown weary of the infinite possibilities potentialities n magnificence that we cood be in our gall to

offend the carriers of racist ideologues hoo
into perpetuity have seen vice as virtue n
crime as normal as compassion n humans as
obscure due to at least in their minds being
born frum unreasonable conception wich
merely served to fuel their universal
wickedness as well as their perversity thru
wich they funneled punishment to the peeple
meaning in shawt our existence was never
meant to be a happy state of affairs butt mah
possession of the truth has frum day one been
equal to these false gods of purloinment thus
i have been hip to the totality of their
unreality of their debased nature altho for
protective purposes until it was time i have
werked hiddenly butt not kiddingly behind
the scenes wit a consecrated sense just
waiting to brang on the retrocession of our
enemies down to even the cancellation of
their shit frum the preceding ages thus
towards the attainment of this end many
thangs have been contributed to mah dna to
produce the results that are now being
wrought in the thoughts of men due to the
essence of mah strong presence for the time to
exalt niggaz to an eternal perpetual
necessary cum up frum this riteous stir of
action that im on cuz i am fo sho on one since
i am placed in the werld to infuse the
doctrine of real spitlosophy into onliest the
readiest yielding minds that are displeased
wit insignificance will see that the
historical deprivation of niggaz is
officially n categorically rejected on earth
as it is in heaven wich are the same when u
kno and i kno u know cuz the fate of the
crackka man plan n his turncoat helpers in
present day is doomed for he had his shawt

time to be loosed upon earth butt has always been incapable and ignorant of embracing solace as salvation thus are sertainly not deserving of divine favors to wit this goes back to mah appearance in the lives of mah niggaz as one hoo was destined to show when least expected in order to be the chief enemy n death of singular kinda white folks hoo were born of decay and has done nuthing butt attack the lives of peeple frum beginning to end so that even the earth is worse off wich is how much they are committed to evil butt one thang bout evil is its subordinate to destiny and i am destiny fashioned to be a hueman being for what must be done to the contrary and much for this reason mah shit is a mystery to the enemy and even sumtimes mah self ion kno how i doo what i doo therewith there is no power in the stars that kan save these fools either especially since their humanity what little there is is not proportionately separate frum their barbarism thus i am well endowed as the consequential feedback unfortunate curse to be unalterably realized unto them as it must happen to them for their irresolute thoughts and actions of their past experiences written down in the niggakashic records of mah memory bank as an elegiac drop to be said as a proper eulogy over the deposit of their ashes wit essential malice as their demise will ring round the werld in the ears so there will be no dout that silly crackkkaz have met their end in the greatest of unhappinesses n expeditiously entombed with all their vain pleasures for their savage state frum wich they were never born to elevate beyond any noticeable degree that is to say the whole of them for it be true that perhaps a miniscule portion of white folks were open to ascendant strains of nobility butt not enuff to save their entire race frum what imma bout to deliver unto that ass fast as a perfeck unfavorable deduction because only death kan be their highest state of kulture since all else is palpable about them as they have hitherto always been as in this werld only sertain white skin is capable of rendering gentility to anutha man thus being smitten is the only god that kan improve their condition whereas since the niggods knew that i am one hoo never waivers nor wood i abandon the path that was set out i will see to it that mah mission is carried out as an occurrence of persecution in order to obtain n attain the perfected outcum of a riteous butt furious man of his peeple hoo has voluntarily been willing to suffer infinite pains n unceaseless struggling when need be by their fallacious assaults upon mah innocent person in an effort to derail n curtail me yet by me being made frum a type a fabrik they dont make no more the mo they ardently tried to deaden mah mission to purge them the more it tightened n intensified mah resolve and mah necessary desire to be extraordinary rather than just ordinary and be a trubble unto them continuously and please note this has been frum mah infancy that i started exhibiting the unavoidable tendency to cause racists the suffering they have caused mah peeple in return so that where ever enjoyment or pleazure was denied niggaz let alone to keep niggaz frum the bare necessities of life for whole hoods n households deteriorate into self hate as part of a consistent theme of tormentation then so

be it to cum back to them thru me as
incovenience thats meant to be detriment &
exterminate their evilarchal species as had
to be made manifest in the manner u are now
reading as an awareness imperative thats been
and becum an examination of mah shituation
over a long period of time as i gained a thoro
unnerstanding of their refined hatred wich
is a definite deviation frum the natural
order of thangs and for that mah sojourn tho a
painful one on many an occasion i wood be
remiss if i did not say this that has just been
said n read for the head for as this has been
mah spitestamental destiny as the nigga i am
to have adopted this cogent maybe even hail
mary strategery to stop their successive
oppressions thus i have spit what I have just
spat under a type of highly necessary
agitated outrage that has never been able to
be palliated nor comforted therefore i have
remained inconsolable and of an invincible
frame of mind forever allergic to restraint n
servitude that has been the wish of the
powerful evil hoo found me incompatible to
their enslavement sentiments that backfired
on them and produced in me only a spirit
beyond the reach of bribery or sellout
stigmitization for i was born frum day one
consecrated n confirmed to recover the minds
n souls of a particular collective crew of
real niggaz frum the demonic artifice the
malevolent plotters against humanity so no
dout i had to cum full strength about past
indignations as i owed it to u dear real
niggaz as the enemy of our enemies wit their
incessant unfair advantages and their
wayward flesh that like fruit had to mature

into the bitch slap that wood cause their fall
this day under mah pimp hand.

ABOUT DuVAY KNOX

DuVay Knox aka the King of the Underground Black Pulp Fiction Novel is the Delta Louisiana/Mississippi-born author of The SOUL COLLECTOR (Creative Onion Press) & The PUSSY DETECTIVE (Clash Books). He specializes in writing gritty/black pulp fiction/black exploitation-themed short stories n novels. He is also the Publisher/Owner of BLACK PULP FICTION PUBLISHING HOUSE specializing in the same type-a-novels he writes.

EMAIL: duvayknox@yahoo.com

SUBSTACK: https://duvay.substack.com/

SOCIALMEDIA:

http://www.twitter.com/duvayknox

Publisher BLACK PULP FICTION PUBLISHING HOUSE

http://www.blackpulpfictionpublishinghouse.com

Bookings & Workshops: Call/Text 314-255-8025

www.ingramcontent.com/pod-product-compliance
Lightning Source LLC
Chambersburg PA
CBHW070636120726
47909CB00004B/1466